Cool from the Waxing Moon

Shoju and Matashi, Book Two

Kon Blacke

DDP
DEEP DESIRES PRESS
Winnipeg, Canada

Copyright © 2024 Kon Blacke
Cover layout copyright © 2024 Story Perfect Dreamscape

This is a work of fiction. Names, characters, business, places, events, and incidents are either products of the author's imagination or used in a fictitious manner. Any resemblances to actual persons, living or dead, or actual events is purely coincidental.

Editor: Margaret Larson

Published June 2024 by Deep Desires Press.

Deep Desires Press
PO Box 51053 Tyndall Park
Winnipeg, Manitoba R2X 3B0
Canada

Visit http://www.deepdesirespress.com for more scorching hot erotica and erotic romance.

Subscribe to our email newsletter to get notified of all our hot new releases, sales, and giveaways! Visit deepdesirespress.com/newsletter to sign up today!

Cool from the Waxing Moon

Author's Note

This boy's love story contains graphic gay sex. It also contains fetishes such as shibari (rope bondage), cum and saliva worship, and vacuum cupping for titillation.

This story also falls under the boy's love Omegaverse umbrella, a genre where men can get pregnant. Omegaverse, even though unique to boys' love, can trace its origins back to Western sci-fi parody stories (fanfiction) and love stories between werewolves and humans.

For this story, I have done my own spin on the boys' love Omegaverse. In it, *all* the men living within the "secret village" can get pregnant—they are all Omegas. But like other stories in this genre, Omegas come into their monthly heat at which time they are then able to be impregnated to bear a child. They have a reproductive organ that functions similar to a uterus within the anal cavity, above where the prostate is located. Only boys are born.

All characters involved in any sexual act or sexual situation are over 18 years of age.

Enjoy Shoju and Matashi's story!

Glossary

In these two Omegaverse stories, I've used the Kami as though they are gods of sorts, living all around in nature—concentrated at the caldera where the secret village lies—from Heaven's high to the ground below.

In truth, the term Kami is far more nebulous in Japanese folklore. It can mean a god or a deity, as I've stated, but it can also be used to describe a force of nature, used to define happenings that can't be explained (such as one's fate), or even an object held sacred or respected which Kami have blessed with their presence, such as a cross or talisman.

Also, some notes on words I've used:

Osumase, the name of the "secret village" that translates to "final" or "end" is from two words, Osugaki and Haramase.

OSUgaki = conceived (Omega)
Hara**MASE** = conceiver (Alpha)

Jussei Island

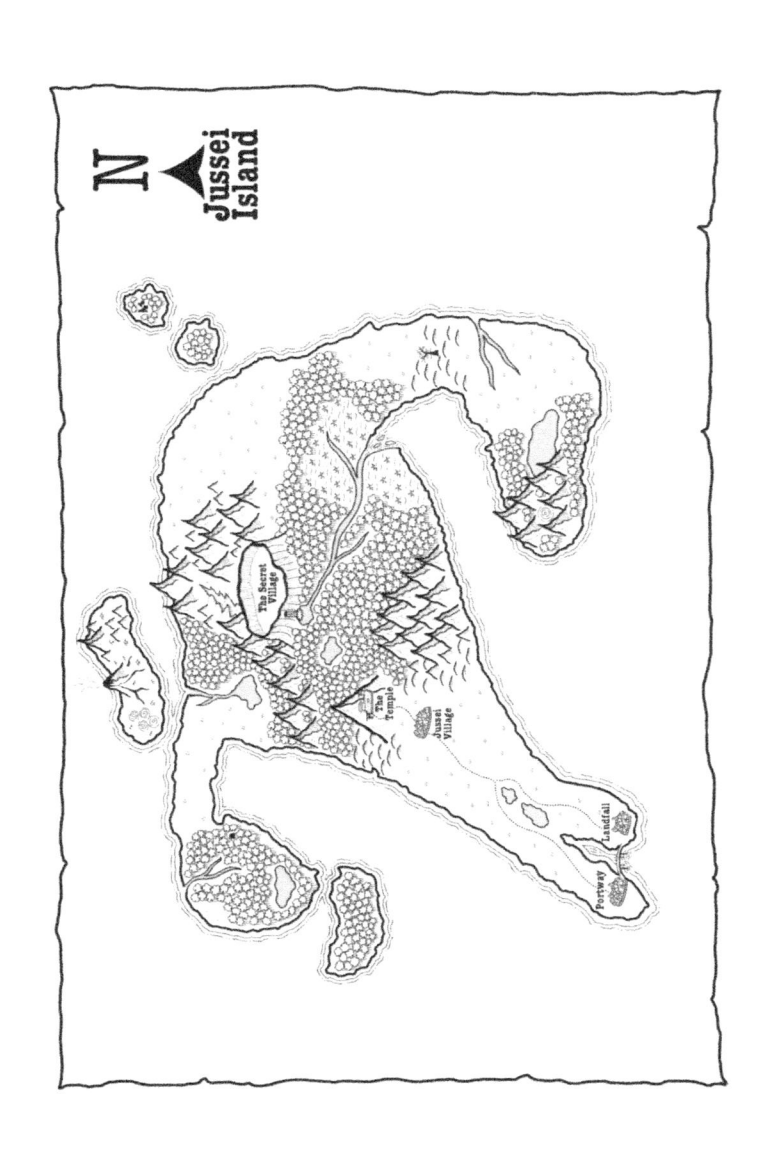

- The Secret Village
- The Temple
- Jussei Village
- Portway
- Landfall

1

Matashi had failed.

Most of all, he'd failed his family, Shoju, Akai, *and* his unborn son. But while he waited for the katana to strike, he didn't weep. He didn't even flinch.

Failures like him deserved to die.

Matashi closed his eyes, his end only moments away. He just wished he'd had more time with Akai. Wished he'd seen his son grow up most of all. But that wouldn't happen now.

"Stop!" a man called, scaring the birds within the branches above;-they took flight with protesting squawks. "Stop, Master Ito! Stop this instant!"

Mat looked up, stunned he'd been saved from the blade's strike by another master—and the creepy Master Fuoco at that.

What was going on?

"How dare you interrupt me, Master Fuoco!" Master Ito fumed, his face reddening, a little vein at his temple pulsing. "How dare you!"

Master Fuoco stood defiantly, hands on hips. "You

know the way of the temple; you've been banging on about it for years."

A moment of intensity flared between the two masters as they glared daggers at each other in a sort of mental standoff. Mat swallowed, knowing the next few moments would determine his fate once and for all.

He held his breath.

Thankfully, Master Ito was the first to relax his stance. To Mat's growing relief, he also lowered his sword. A moment of reprieve…or the calm before the storm?

No matter, Mat breathed.

"You're right, of course," the man said as a different kind of expression fell over his face like a dark shadow.

At the same time, Master Fuoco heaved a breath and smiled, even if it was more a sneer that looked like a jagged scar than anything else. Mat became curious. Because, along with his growing nerves about what was going on here, there was certainly more to be told.

A lot more.

Although, he had a feeling that however this played out, it wouldn't bode well for anyone: him, Akai, or Kale.

The next words out of Master Fuoco's mouth confirmed his suspicions. His stomach knotted, and his heart quickened. The storm was approaching in earnest, it seemed, dark and ominous. "You know a captured breeding pair must be placed into the service of the temple."

Master Ito's lips curled into a cruel smile, replacing an already macabre sneer. "Indeed."

"Which one is the outcast's Omega, then?" Master Fuoco asked while sliding his gaze between Akai and Kale, that awful smile of his widening, reflecting the other master's expression perfectly. "Do you know?"

The looks on the masters' faces chilled him.

"I do. It's *that one* there who's mated to Matashi." Master Ito stabbed his bony finger at Akai. "The handsome one with the blue eyes that reflect his defiance."

"He won't be defiant for long." A snort from Master Fuoco. "Bring them both," he ordered the guards, who roughly pulled Mat and Akai up to their feet immediately. "The other Omega…you can do with him as you please, Master Ito. Kill him if that's your desire."

"It *is* my desire to see blood spilled this day."

Mat's stomach tightened even more. Within a blink of an eye, Master Ito struck, his katana thrumming as it sliced through the air with a blur of speed and strength. The terrible sound was followed by a wet, dull thud onto the leaf litter of the forest. At first, Mat was stunned. Stunned! That was until he realised the full ramifications of what had happened.

Kale was dead—just like that.

Beheaded.

"You're a fucking monster!" Mat spat, feeling his throat tighten as grief struck him harder. "You murdered Kale! Murdered him! He…he didn't even get the chance to mate with anyone, either! You…you monster!"

Akai had already burst into tears, collapsing onto the ground, shoulders heaving. Mat wanted to go to him, comfort him, but was yanked away from his lover, his Omega, his man, by the two temple guards who held him.

The guards grabbed Akai again.

Mat, unable to do anything else, felt his eyes sting.

"Ahh, I so enjoyed that," Master Ito said, casually wiping Kale's blood off the blade with a cloth one of the guards had given him. "It made me so very hard." He rubbed his groin to emphasise his words.

Mat's stomach turned even more.

"I can tell you *did* enjoy that, Master Ito," Master Fuoco observed.

Master Ito came to stand in front of Mat, looking down at him with what was unmistakeably disgust. "After killing that filthy Omega friend of yours, outcast, I need a willing boy to fuck. One who'll beg me to blow my load deep into his guts to complete the glory that is this day. Would you be such a boy, hmm?"

"Go *fuck* yourself!" Mat spat as his emotions, his grief for Kale, and the hopeless situation they'd found themselves in swirled within him, threatening to consume him.

"You're a defiant one as well." Master Ito's eyebrows rose. "Perhaps we should have chosen you instead of Shoju as our honoured? I would have enjoyed breaking you in."

Mat felt sick, bile rising to sour the back of his tongue, wanting nothing more than to pull the man's sword from its scabbard to stab him a thousand times with it. Then, when he was dead on the ground, a thousand times more, until he became fit for nothing but mincemeat for the worms.

But Mat couldn't move, being both restrained and weak with sorrow. Besides, he was also too consumed by what had transpired. How he'd ended up like this. Because when he thought about it, if Shoju hadn't left the temple when he had, the masters and guards wouldn't have been out in the forest.

Some turn of fate, indeed.

With his vision blurring and hiccups wracking his body, Mat also found he couldn't speak. He was in too much of a mess to do anything, including swearing in defiance anymore.

Mat quickly resigned himself to the fact that he was beaten. He knew these evil men would do with him as they pleased. His and Akai's life would be nothing more than a living hell from now on. He knew that to his soul. But he also realised something else then.

Something profound.

He wasn't a failure as he had first thought because to fail meant he had to have first tried. No. He was useless. Useless because he could do nothing now to prevent whatever happened next.

Nothing.

Not even to help Akai.

"I'll join you," Master Fuoco said, bringing Mat back to the moment, the horror of the situation coming into focus once more. "And I believe we can choose another honoured from the selected temple servants before they get castrated tonight."

"A good idea," Master Ito said, his leer returning. "I liked how that boy…what's his name? Daiki? Yes, that's it. Daiki Ugomari. I liked how he showed great…potential."

To one of the guards who'd been holding Kale, now standing there with nothing to do no thanks to the poor man being murdered, Master Fuoco ordered, "Get to the temple as quickly as you can to inform Master Vitus that we want Daiki as our new honoured before his balls get cut off. Have him taken to tatami room four as well. We'll begin the three trials with him as soon as he's been affected enough by the herbs within the brazier's smoke."

"Yes, Master," the guard replied immediately with a bow before running toward the rejection gate.

Mat felt sorry for Daiki.

He felt sorry for all of them caught within the evil of the temple masters. Him and Akai most of all.

Master Ito's next words brought their fate into even greater clarity.

"And as for you, outcast," he began, "you'll be locked in a cage away from your Omega until your son is born. After that, you'll be allowed to put another one into him." His laugh echoed and sent a chill all through Mat. "Because from now on, you'll give us your sons to serve the temple as we see fit."

Shoju was already exhausted, sweat dripping off his soaking wet hair, a stitch in his sides. He was breathing hard, too hard, before he'd even run a few hundred meters away from the temple's imposing walls. Was it just from his frenzied sprint from the temple? Or was fear at play here, too?

"I'm t-too…unfit to r-run any…more," Shoju cried,

knowing it was the excess weight that he carried to blame—why did his mum have to be such a great cook? And even though his upbringing was strict, why did she have to dote over him so, too? "Horo…*please*…I need to r-rest!"

Horo went to Shoju straight away.

Which was just as well. Shoju had fallen to his knees, gulping for air like a landed fish. The forest around him spun, his blurry vision making him feel giddy. He could also feel his pulse pound in his ears. Or was that the sound of his heart about to give out because of his exertion?

"We can't rest yet, so I shall carry you, my heart," Horo announced.

"I'll only…s-slow you d-down." Shoju tried to stand. He wobbled. He couldn't get up; his legs were too weak. "Just give me a m-minute, and I'll be able…able to g-go on. Okay?"

More desperately, Horo said, "We mustn't stop." He couldn't hide his worried glance. "We haven't gone far enough for the temple guards to give up the chase."

"How much…f-farther must w-we go before they…do give up?"

Itsuki and Shin approached. They both held worried expressions, heavier than Horo's, to be honest. Shoju's guilt prickled at the nape of his neck; he didn't like how he was holding them up because of his physical failings. He added a weak, "Sorry," to all of them, feeling it was needed.

Then he hung his head.

Horo gently grabbed his chin so they could look into each other's eyes. "Please don't apologise, Shoju. And don't worry. Over the next rise, I believe there's a pool that's hidden enough for us to be safe for a moment or two before we continue."

Holding hands now, Shin and Itsuki agreed.

Shoju was about to protest, not wanting to be a burden to anyone, least of all himself, when he heard shouts coming from the hazy, humid distance beyond the thick trees behind them.

He swallowed…hard.

No doubt the ruckus was from the temple guards pursuing them. Who else could it be? Village hunters never ventured too close to temple lands for fear of upsetting the Kami of the forest. Or, more than likely, disturbing the supernatural being who lived here…so they believed.

And whether the ghosts and demons of stories were real or imagined, Shoju wasn't sure. Although, he had a fair idea the secret village of the Omegas where they were heading probably had a lot to do with sowing the seeds of rumour when it came to trying to keep others away.

The village was a secret for a reason.

Not even Shoju had heard of it until now. And besides, good monster stories were good monster stories. If nothing else, they frightened children into behaving themselves. As Shoju had been, when his mum had told him of a nasty goblin who liked to wear the skins of boys who misbehaved too much.

"If you don't do as you're told this instant, young man, the goblin will stalk you in the night," his mum had warned when he'd moaned about brushing his teeth one evening. "And when he catches you, he'll then peel off your skin while you're still alive and kicking, he will."

"How does he know where I live?" Shoju was only six years old at the time, he remembered.

"He knows," she'd added sternly. "Goblins are like that. Nosy and nasty and with a keen nose that can smell boys misbehaving from the top of the mountain beyond the protection of the temple."

"I'll…umm, go brush my teeth, then, Mum."

"There's a good boy."

Shoju shivered; the thought of that goblin was still frightening to him. And from that day on, he was always a good boy. Doing everything he was told without question, no matter who demanded it of him. From the elders of the village to his companion Matashi, he did what he was told.

He *was* a good son, too.

Perhaps that's why Shoju still needed to do as he was told, even as an adult. Still needed other people's validation. He therefore understood all too well why he'd let the masters of the temple do what they wanted to him without protest, and it really didn't have too much to do with being chosen as their honoured or the good life his mother would have because of it.

His blind obedience had been indoctrinated into him.

But even though that could be seen as a weakness, had been by many, in fact, Shoju didn't think of it that way. Not at all. Obedience was his strength, and one day he'd get to prove it.

One day.

"We've got to go! Now!" Horo said, knocking Shoju from his reverie while he still recovered from the sprint, his breathing slowly evening even if sweat dripped off his nose.

To Shoju, there was no doubt about his man's desperation; he felt it, too. Therefore, before he could blink, Horo moved to pick him up off the leaf litter without asking permission.

"Hey!" Shoju complained weakly as he was held in Horo's strong arms.

"It's this or be captured."

Shoju sighed. But as he put his arm around Horo's neck for better comfort, suddenly feeling his closeness, his love and concern for him most of all, he relaxed. "I'm glad…you're here with me."

"I wouldn't want it any other way."

Horo carried Shoju without too much worry, even though the terrain was rough. Itsuki and Shin walked ahead, checking the ground for any dangers. Being held like this brought him into Horo's world even more.

Shoju realised he loved it.

Soon, the shouting that had been coming closer seemed to fall far, far behind them until unable to be heard. Perhaps the guards had given up. Shoju relaxed further, even managing a smile as he cuddled into Horo, kissing his neck. A groan of approval was Shoju's reward.

After they'd gone some distance, Shoju had to ask, "Do you think I'm weak, Horo?"

"Not at all. Why?"

Shoju had to think carefully for a moment. "Because of my…privileged but strict upbringing…most folks consider my obedience a weakness. And I…I wanted to know what you thought, that's all."

Horo stopped. "Obedience isn't a weakness at all. Far from it, my heart."

"Then it's a strength?" Shoju asked hopefully. "As I believe it is."

"It's far more than that."

"How so?"

Horo carefully put Shoju down. He could stand now, breathe more easily, and he felt better for the rest he'd received, even if only for a little while. He clasped his man's hand immediately, enjoying the continuation of their contact.

They walked on together.

Horo answered once Shin and Itsuki came into sight. They'd just passed a thicket of dense, ancient trees, Shin gesturing for them to hurry. "Obedience with a pure heart behind it, like you have, Shoju, is about honour and the respect underlying it. It is those attributes which are considered the highest and most noble to have. That's also why I fell in love with you."

"You mean that?"

"I do."

Shoju wasn't convinced that was the end of it but was satisfied for now. After all, even if he had honour in spadefuls as well as the respect of others aplenty because of who he was, that didn't necessarily mean they saw him any differently.

They still saw him as being weak, he knew.

What could he do to convince them that a good boy, spoiled by life and always loved, was also someone to take seriously? Because when it came down to it, that's how Shoju felt.

That he was never taken seriously.

He felt he needed to explain such things to Horo because the man was going to be his husband, and there should be no secrets between them. No doubts either, imagined or otherwise. Before he could, they came to the promised pool.

It was beautiful.

Not only did branches of weeping willows drink from the sparkling waters, there was abundant wildlife everywhere, from deer to fish to birds; drinking, swimming, and flying all around the protected sanctuary they'd found themselves within.

Shoju took in a breath.

Shin and Itsuki had disrobed—including stripping off their fundoshi—to jump into the water, splashing and larking about seconds later. Shoju found it amusing how they soon wrestled, playing the game where the first to touch their opponent's balls was declared the winner of that round.

A common game.

Shoju remembered how a lot of boys in the village he grew up in wrestled like that at the public baths, including Matashi with his other friends. Not that Shoju participated in such things if he could help it. He tried to avoid the baths at the best of times, being so self-conscious of his weight.

Matashi always tried to encourage him to attend. And once again, because of his obedience, would only do so if

COOL FROM THE WAXING MOON 13

asked, even if he felt uncomfortable, and the other boys stared at him. Some even laughed behind their hands.

"Did you want me to bathe you, Shoju?" Horo asked, again bringing Shoju back to the moment.

After his run, Shoju realised he would like that a lot. They were out of immediate danger, but his thoughts were spiralling. As he looked upon his man drenched in sunlight, all handsome and lovely, dandelion seeds dancing around him, too, a different urge overtook him.

With lust growing in his voice like ink slowly staining calm water, he said, "I *would* like that…but only if you fuck me first."

A lovely smile came over Horo's face, one that made Shoju weak in the knees. "I think you'll need a bath first; you're still sweaty from all that running."

Shoju didn't feel like obeying as he felt himself harden. "You've given me your saliva and cum every time you've laid me down, so why can't you lick my sweat from my balls before you stick your cock in me?"

Horo raised an eyebrow. "Is this coming from what we spoke about earlier?"

"Yes, it is," Shoju admitted.

Horo offered a bow. "Then it'll be my pleasure to do as you ask of me, my heart. I want nothing else but for you to be happy and satisfied."

Shoju was taken aback. "I'm sorry, but, umm…will *you* be satisfied because you're doing this for me? Even if you may not like doing it?"

"Again, you don't need to apologise." Horo grabbed Shoju's other hand, pulling him close, so close his man's breath tickled him on his quivering lips. "Because I *will* lick you all over. I'll give you everything—for my tongue, my mouth, my cock, and my body are yours to pleasure you. Always. And pleasing *you* is *my* pleasure. Never forget that."

"Then…then give me everything we both desire, please."

"Yes, Shoju, my heart."

From there, carefully and with a quivering urgency, Horo lay Shoju down on the sandy shore. The hunger for his man consumed Shoju as his shadow overtook everything else. But most of all, Shoju became overwhelmed by sudden heat as fingers delicately caressed him to make him shiver delightfully all over.

Without thought, Shoju opened his mouth, sticking out his tongue as far as it would go, the desperate need to taste Horo's saliva shockingly and wonderfully real.

A smile from Horo.

A moment of teasing, too, before he dribbled what Shoju desired, wetting his tongue even more than it already was because of his arousal and his need for Horo.

"Mhm, yes." Shoju writhed after swallowing.

"And that's just the beginning, I promise." A kiss was given—deep, sloppy, and sucking—just how Shoju craved it.

How he loved it.

Shoju moaned even more while their lips were connected, while Horo's hands grabbed him with more purpose. They became one, their rhythms merging to synchronise, including their breathing.

When they parted, gasping, trembling, Shoju, tingling

delightfully all over, whispered, "Take off my clothes and lick me all over. Leave your trails of saliva all over my skin to map out your love for me."

"As you desire, my heart."

No other words needed to be spoken between them as Horo removed his clothing. As asked. As demanded, really. As soon as his fundoshi was unwrapped, his cock sprang to attention. Shoju was ready.

Achingly so.

Shoju arched his back, heart lurching as he moved so he could expose his neck for his man, feeling vulnerable but trusting him all at the same time. Horo kissed and licked it, most of all in the places below Shoju's ears that sent even greater shivers all through him. He was on fire, the bright embers within him burning only for Horo.

"Yes!" Shoju encouraged.

Horo lifted Shoju's arms to pin them above his head. "You smell so strongly of your sweat."

"Does it…bother you?" Shoju's cheeks warmed.

"No! Not at all." The dance of Horo's tongue then begun deep in Shoju's armpit, the sensations of that action intensifying quickly. He realised his body would soon be ready for his man to use, and that thought thrilled him. "It makes you more manly, and I adore that as I adore you," he added as Shoju began to climb toward ecstasy already.

And that surprised him.

Because not only did strange and wonderful sensations overtake him as Horo's tongue licked away his sweat from the crevices of his pits in long lashes that both tickled and aroused, a few times—and to Shoju's amusement—Horo's attention got kind of tangled within his little tuft of pit hair before it was wetted down.

After Shoju was cleaned in that way, so hot and sexy, he received another kiss. Indeed, he begged for it by opening his mouth wider, tongue lolling once more for his man to worship. And worship it, Horo did. The taste of himself was strong as it mixed with Horo's plentiful drool. Shoju loved it and became even harder for his man.

Very hard.

"Keep…keep licking me!" Shoju said, with wanting groans between sloppy kisses that made him giddy. "Get me so willing that…that I'll cum as soon as you s-stick your dick in me!"

A smile before Horo moved onto the other armpit. From there, his attention moved lower and lower: nipples, chest, stomach, and navel. By the time Horo began licking Shoju's pubes in long lashes, his cock and balls, too, really getting into it, moaning and slurping, another need overtook Shoju: the need to have his ass worshipped in the way the rest of him had been. He opened his legs, holding himself so Horo could do what he wanted without hindrance.

"Get your tongue…right into my sweaty hole, please!" he gasped.

An agreeable groan of understanding from Horo. Of desire, too, if Shoju wasn't mistaken. Before he could even *think* of questioning Horo's feelings on the matter—or wonder what being rimmed would really feel like—he was being treated—no, worshipped—in a way he'd never experienced before.

Shoju melted under such attention. "Oh…by the gods!" he couldn't help but cry as different tingles and sensations overwhelmed him.

Horo's tongue, a marvel before, was now an instrument of Shoju's fantasies. Being licked down there affected him in a deep and profound way, like he was a treasure to his man, and nothing was out of bounds to discover now that he'd been mapped by his tongue. As Horo's ministrations continued, the sensations Shoju was feeling intensified to the point where he couldn't do much else but be taken along for the ride.

So good.

And did he ride Horo's tongue? Yes, he did. Shoju moved with the action, groaning and writhing under such intense, intimate attention. And to make it even better, to Shoju's surprise, Horo's tongue soon penetrated him after really wetting his entrance. Then he spit on him down there like he'd done into Shoju's mouth.

That was different!

Shoju shuddered. "Oh…"

To feel Horo's dripping drool after he'd been prepared by his tongue—such a warm wonder, too—to feel it go as deep as it could, to rim him from the inside as well as the outside, that was something special.

Something wonderful and intimate, truly.

Shoju, his body a mess now, quivering while he writhed, was lost for words. He could only manage animalistic noises deep from his throat as he threw his head back in ecstasy. And make them he did.

He was Horo's.

When Shoju did manage to speak, he was already close to climax. Too close. He cried out to his man, "Fuck me n-now, Horo! Fuck me h-hard! I *need* you!"

What was asked for was done without delay.

Once more, Horo's shadow came over him. Shoju opened his mouth again as Horo's cock pierced his willing and wanting ass, right to the root of it, with an almighty thrust. Shoju moaned, loving it as a stab of pleasurable pain shot through him, making him gulp.

Horo quickly gained his rhythm.

Shoju loved the idea of his man consuming him as he did: body, mind, and soul. And yes, that also worked both ways. Shoju completed Horo, he knew.

Such a thought got him even more worked up. So much so, he was clawing at Horo's back, moaning, shuddering and groaning, along with plenty more wet kisses.

Kisses enhanced by his own taste.

What's more, Shoju was achingly big. So hard. So beautiful. As big as Horo—who now filled him perfectly—was.

Like they were always meant to be.

Shoju couldn't imagine himself with any other, not even Matashi, now. And that was a profound thought. A wonderful one, too, because, yes, he was as needy for Horo as Horo was for him.

They almost growled at each other as their passion heightened.

It was bloody brilliant.

All because Horo, his man ten years his senior, experienced and caring at the same time, met Shoju's every desire so willingly and without condition. And even though Shoju was a virgin before Horo, that didn't mean he didn't know how he wanted to be treated. He wanted love. And to be loved so deeply by a first lover? That was the best feeling.

Shoju would do anything for Horo.

He'd even die for him.

"Kiss me!" he begged once Horo began to grunt with more purpose, his thrusting harder and more determined.

Sweat dripped. Cheeks reddened. Shoju had wrapped his legs around his man, pulling him so he went deeper and came closer. So close, they shared their intoxicating heat and gasping breaths along with everything else, including each other's space and time.

A moment of pause while Horo must have taken in what Shoju had asked of him. "You don't mind me kissing you after I've rimmed you?"

Shoju couldn't give two hoots of a barn owl about that. "I desire your wet kisses—I don't care where your mouth's been on me!"

No other words were needed.

Shoju was soon consumed by Horo's mouth as much as anything else. And, yes, the taste of himself was once more potent, stronger and more pungent than before, but he didn't care. He loved it. Loved how Horo had licked him all over. And now they shared that act of love in the most intimate way possible.

It was heaven.

All too soon—or was it after an eternity?—Shoju came with almighty shudders that shook him to his bones. Sucking in air in heaving breaths, arching his back, begging for more kisses at the same time, so hot and sweating again, dribbling saliva as much as Horo did, he let himself go completely.

Shoju came and came.

Horo did, too.

For another age, they remained together on the shore, connected as lovers, true lovers, could only be. And as Shoju cooled in his man's arms, staring into his eyes, feeling loved above all else, he realised something else that amused him.

He giggled.

"What do you find so funny?" Horo asked.

Shoju, feeling heat in his cheeks once more, said, "I think I'd like you to take me into the water to wash me now."

An eyebrow rose, along with a curious look. "What's so amusing about that? I want to bathe you and will do so while I keep my kisses upon you, as I said I would."

He cheekily replied, "Yeah, but thanks to you, I'm even dirtier now." The stickiness of the thick ribbons of ejaculation was all over his stomach and then some, right to his collarbones.

"That I can see." Horo smiled right to his deep, dark, and mysterious browns.

When Shoju moved, the unmistakable sensation of Horo's love oozing out of him overtook everything else. But that wasn't the reason for his amusement, and he added to clarify, "I think I've got sand in places that'll soon chafe me if I don't get rid of it soon." Another giggle. "I bet my balls look like little daigaku imo, huh!"

Horo, after looking down, laughed in obvious

agreement. "You're right." He got up to offer his hand to Shoju. "They sure do resemble sugar-coated sweet potatoes. But it's also rather cute."

Shoju admitted he loved how Horo saw him. Because no matter how he felt, getting down on himself many times as he'd wrestled with his weight throughout his life, his man clearly thought of him as a better person than he did.

And that was perhaps more profound than being in love. To Shoju, anyway. Mostly because it meant Horo didn't hold any conditions against him for the love he gave. And that, above all else, was attractive and sexy and oh so brilliant.

More giggles, Shoju unable to help himself after his thoughts. "Then you'd better get the sand off me before I put my fundoshi back on, right?"

"Agreed."

Horo and Shoju walked to the lapping water's edge hand in hand, the insects buzzing and birds chirping, the day bright all around them. It was a beautiful moment. Tender, too. Shoju, even though lost in his own world while in Horo's presence, noticed Itsuki and Shin intertwined in the clear water, sharing their own passion.

Horo added, "Can I carry you into the pool, my heart?"

"Yes, please."

Horo once more easily picked up Shoju. From there, he remained within his man's hold, loved and adored as he was washed with tender, loving hands all over him. He was kissed many, many times, too.

Shoju could get used to this.

Within the water, Shoju was touched, kissed, washed,

and worshipped, and he felt the most at peace he'd ever felt in his life. It was a peace that calmed his soul and made his heart yearn even more for Horo. Unfortunately, he didn't get too much time to get comfortable within his man's hold.

Without warning, Itsuki, after being loved by Shin as Shoju had been loved by Horo on that shore this day, came over to them, looking flustered and flushed.

"What is it, my friend?" Horo asked, concern on his face.

Itsuki pointed to the trees beyond the pool's edge, nervousness clear in his gesture as he shook. "Shin says he heard voices coming from over there, just beyond the tree line."

Horo sucked in a breath, mumbling something crude.

Shoju, startled, anxious, and a whole lot of scared, got up as quickly as he could when Horo let him go. "Have the…have the guards found us?"

Horo's expression grew darker, even as he remained stern and imposing. "We must hide."

Shin joined them, grabbing Itsuki's hand. "Where can we hide out here in the open, Master Horo?"

Shoju, quickly scanning the area, noticed a rocky outcrop beyond the willow trees. Hopefully not too far away to flee to without being seen.

"How about over there?" he suggested.

Too late.

For it was in that moment—a moment of held breaths and worry for not only himself but Horo and his new friends—that Shoju heard what Shin had claimed to.

Voices. And they were getting louder, too.

But what worried Shoju the most, aside from being naked and exposed, was that they were all defenceless. They were also outnumbered. No sooner had their situation dawned on him than six men emerged from the undergrowth to stand ominously on the shore. Six big, strong, burly men who held weapons, too, from katanas to bows.

They weren't temple guards, though.

So, who were they?

Horo, as observant as Shoju, placed his hands on his hips. "Who are you who dares disturb us?"

Shoju would have found that admirable, except for one thing. The tallest, a blond-haired man with an impressive blond moustache and beard,-stepped forward. "Who we are is of no concern, but we should kill you all where you stand for desecrating our sacred waters."

2

Mat's treatment wasn't good.

Not that he expected anything less. Not for him. But his heart broke for Akai, because, as an Omega, they treated him worst of all. Not only was his cage smaller, he was given far less food and water.

Which Mat found kind of strange seeing as Akai was pregnant; he'd need all the nutrition he could get soon enough. Sooner, no doubt. If there was anything Mat understood from his large family upbringing, the first few months inside the womb were the most important.

"Are you…okay?" was all Mat could feebly ask. His fear for Akai, the hopelessness of the situation, made him sick to his stomach.

Akai only cried in reply, hands to his face while he knelt on the cage's straw-covered floor. He'd been like that since Kale was beheaded by Master Ito. The master had acted as if the man meant nothing to him—which, being an Omega, Kale didn't, Mat supposed.

Mat's heart ached terribly.

But what made him feel worst of all was the fact that even though they were shoved into cages side by side so they could see each other, they couldn't touch. Couldn't even brush fingertips no matter how far Mat tried to reach.

"It's hopeless," he declared after almost hurting himself, his armpit and shoulder pressed against the metal bars as he tried to touch Akai, to comfort him.

He couldn't even do that.

Mat sighed deeply with regret. He was fucking useless in every way.

"There is always h-hope," Akai said through his emotions without looking up.

Mat didn't know how to respond. What was hopeful about their situation? Nothing. They were both being treated like animals. Worse than that, even! Because being used as a breeding pair for the temple was a living nightmare.

Mat thought of their unborn son.

He shivered…terribly.

He couldn't think of anything worse than being forced into servitude from birth. That wasn't a life. But what could he do to prevent the masters from taking their son or any future ones? Again, nothing. Because Mat knew to his bones that he couldn't resist Akai's heat when he came into it. The first time it had happened, he'd not lasted long before the urge to mate took over, until it was all he could think about.

Yet, he had to hold on to some small hope, as Akai suggested. As such, Mat became determined to do one thing.

He had to escape.

And not just escape, but take Akai and all the other

boys with him. All of them, including their new honoured, Daiki, who were caught within the temple master's evil through no fault of their own. Lured with false pretences and false promises.

Mat then thought of Shoju…and Master Ito's words.

"Oh, didn't you know?" Master Ito had cooed. "Shoju and his caretaker escaped the temple with their house servants early this morning. You just missed them. Again, what a shame you didn't cross paths. It would have saved you a lot of bother. Isn't it delicious how fate works, hmm?"

And if what Master Ito had said was true—which Mat didn't doubt because it was to the Master's advantage to speak truthfully—that meant Shoju *was* free.

That was something.

And if Shoju had escaped because of a sympathiser within the temple's ranks, that meant there could be another like this caretaker of his here.

Perhaps more than one.

Hopefully.

As if to answer his thoughts, a servant approached; he was holding a tray of food and water, eyes downcast. Mat recognised him as being one of his older brother's friends. Gorou was his name.

The access window to the cage was unlocked with a metallic clank, and the tray was pushed onto the ledge for Mat to take.

"Here's your lunch," Gorou said distantly, still not looking up.

Mat swallowed as a realisation fell upon him. Gorou was far different from what he remembered. Before, he was always the larrikin, the one leading the way into mischief for the group he hung around with, including Mat's brother, Ryuu. But now…

Now he seemed timid and defeated.

Of course, Mat only knew Gorou before he'd come of age. Before the elders of the village had chosen Ryuu and Gorou for the temple. And that was the cruellest fate of all. Ryuu hadn't been seen since being named outcast, while Gorou…he clearly wasn't the same.

He was broken; there was no other word for it.

Mat felt deeply sad for him. "Thanks," was all he said in reply.

"It's Matashi Soju, isn't it?" Gorou asked.

"Yes, that's me." Mat decided to elaborate, needing to know where Gorou stood. "You used to know my older brother, Ryuu."

Gorou then looked up, profound sadness in his eyes as a spark of a memory must have stuck him. "Ryuu?"

"Yes. Ryuu. He was blond-haired and tall and growing a beard." Mat's stomach knotted when he realised that he'd referred to his brother in the past tense, but he pressed on. "You were his best friend, Gorou. Remember?"

The blank expression still held. "Sorry, I don't remember." But despite what Gorou said, Mat saw a glint of recognition behind his dull, sad eyes.

Instinctively, Mat reached out to touch the man. "That's okay. But you remembered me, so that's something, right?"

Gorou pulled away before contact was made. "I don't know you."

"You do. You said my name before."

A shake of his head, his look distant once more. "Who are you, again?"

Mat sighed, deciding to take a different turn. "It doesn't matter who I am, does it? All you need to know is that I'm someone who needs your help, Gorou. Can you help me and Akai? Can you?"

Gorou slowly looked at Akai, then back at Mat. "You don't need my help." A dark expression replaced the earlier one of defeat. But it wasn't a cruel look, not like the ones the masters held onto like they held their privileged positions within the temple.

"Yes. Yes, we do." Mat swallowed, wanting to get his desperation across without begging. He failed. "We're going to be treated worse than animals in these cages if we don't get out soon. Please, you've got to help us. If not for us, then for the boys…the *sons* they'll take from us. *Please*."

"Those boys will be treated better than any servant—the last boy born inside the temple became a master." Gorou snorted, that time in disgust; he clearly hated the masters.

Mat understood completely.

"No," Gorou continued. "When you're a servant, if that's your fate as it had been mine, you have your balls replaced by eons-worn stones from the bottom of the chōzuya fountain after initiation. From there, you're raped every day simply because you're a convenient hole for the master's cocks to be warmed within. You're tortured for their amusement, too."

Mat felt terrible. "I'm sorry…I didn't know."

"Who does outside these walls?"

And right there was the deepest truth of all of this. Within the sacred high walls surrounding the temple, the masters did as they pleased to those who served them, the villagers and elders unaware they were sending their chosen boys to a life of hell.

Mat swallowed again. "I'm so sorry about what's happened to you, really."

"You know nothing." Gorou turned his back on Mat. "How could you? You were named an outcast and became one of the fortunate until you were stupid enough to return."

"I came back to rescue my companion, Shoju," Mat explained, as if doing so would prove he wasn't foolish but honourable.

He knew it didn't, though.

"Then you're also a fool if you think any of us can be released from the iron grip of the masters of this terrible place."

"Shoju did," Mat pointed out. "He escaped."

"Then he's the worst fool of them all. Worse than even you, for he was honoured, and now he'll be less than nothing because of what he did if they see him again. Less than even me, a mere servant." Another snort from Gorou, one full of an even greater derision. "But for his sake, let's hope he doesn't follow your path and return. He's not an Alpha or Omega, so he really won't be of any use to them now that they've chosen Daiki as their new honoured."

"Being an honoured means to be sacrificed," Mat said. "How can that be anything better than being a servant or a guard here?"

"Because," Gorou shot back, "I'd rather have a year of

being worshipped and admired, my every desire met before my end, than a lifetime of misery, abuse, and rape after being mutilated."

Mat felt terrible again. "I'm so sorry."

Gorou walked away without saying another word. A long moment of silence followed, except for Akai's crying, now softer but no less heartbreaking to hear.

To no one but still out loud, Mat said, "There goes our only chance at hope."

Akai stirred. "Perhaps," he whispered through his sorrow in reply. "Perhaps not."

"What do you mean?"

"If we…" A moment of pause. "Maybe there's something we can offer Gorou? He may then…help us, after all. Perhaps."

"What could we offer him?"

Akai looked up, right into Mat's eyes; the love they shared, clear as day, lived within those beautiful blues of his without condition. Mat's heart yearned once more. He needed to hold his man so badly it hurt. Damn these fucking cages preventing him from doing so.

Damn everything.

"That *is* the question, isn't it?" Akai said.

***

Shoju, momentarily recovering from the shock of being

confronted by the hunters of the secret village—because who else could they be?—believed he recognised their leader.

"Is that…is that you, Ryuu?" he asked tentatively.

Ryuu studied Shoju for a moment before a dawning realisation took over his previously stern disposition. "Shoju? Are you serious? Is that you? Little Shoju, who couldn't be separated from my little brother, no matter what?"

"Yes, that's right, it's me!" Shoju said, now delighted he was not only recognised, but he'd found Mat's long-lost older brother. What had it been? Two years now? Maybe more since Ryuu was declared an outcast. "And I have grown up a bit since then, as you can see."

"I can." A smile as Ryuu's gaze wandered over Shoju. "But what are you doing here with that temple filth, pray tell?"

Shoju turned to where Ryuu gestured with a jutting chin. "He's not—"

Horo put his arm around Shoju's shoulder, halting his words. It was then Horo spoke, calmly and quietly. "Ryuu knows who I am because of my cut cock, Shoju. It's not exactly hard to hide it when I'm standing naked before him, now is it?"

Ryuu laughed. "Even without the protection of your guards surrounding you, you hold such arrogance in your voice that it brings bile up from my stomach to burn my throat."

"I wasn't trying to be arrogant," Horo protested.

Shoju could feel the tension build; he didn't like it. Instinctively, he came to stand in front of Horo.

Thankfully, before things ignited into a terrible situation, another man, one Shoju immediately saw as being heavily pregnant, stepped forward from behind the others to grab a hold of Ryuu's hand.

"It's all right, my husband," the man said with a gentle, defusing voice. He was beautiful to Shoju, stunningly so with his rosy cheeks, calm face, and a shock of spiky red hair that dominated everything else. In fact, because of the blazing sun coming to its zenith above, it looked as though there was a fire atop his head. "Don't you recognise our saviour?"

Ryuu opened and closed his mouth for a moment before uttering, "By the Kami who protect us all, I'm so sorry I didn't recognise you, Master Horo." He then bowed, one done in apology, Shoju believed.

At least the tension had dissipated, thank goodness!

Relieved somewhat, that's when Shoju turned to see Horo smile and bow low in response. It seemed Ryuu was forgiven. A good thing, too. Mostly because Shoju was worried things could have escalated if Ryuu's husband hadn't intervened, to all of their detriment. As in, ending their lives with sharp objects thrust into them kind of detriment.

So, yes, Shoju was glad it hadn't come to that; he preferred being alive as opposed to any other state of being. He had too much to live for now that he'd found such profound love with Horo, even more than he'd felt for Mat, if he was being honest.

Horo added, "I'm always at your service, my friend. Yours and any others who need my help."

Ryuu, holstering his bow behind his back, replied, "Again, I'm sorry I didn't recognise you at first. Will you ever forgive me?"

Horo chuckled. "You were too busy looking at my status to be concerned with anything else, am I correct?"

Ryuu stood at attention, his cheeks burning bright red, as red as his husband's hair, if not more so. "What can I do to make up for my mistake?"

Horo winked. "Well, how about you join us for a cool down before you then take us to your village? That's where we were headed before you interrupted us."

Another bow in respect. "It shall be done."

Ryuu's husband chimed in, "Since Ryuu has become too embarrassed, he's forgotten the etiquette of our occasion, so it would seem. Please allow *me* to introduce us. My name is Mikaro, and this here is…" Mikaro gestured to the other four men in turn as he said their names.

Shoju didn't hear them; he was too pre-occupied with something else. Something he'd never have believed if he hadn't seen it with his own eyes. "How far…how long have you been pregnant for, Mikaro?" he had to ask before he burst.

Mikaro beamed a smile, looking lovingly at Ryuu. "I'm seven months into our second pregnancy, aren't I, my husband?"

"That you are."

Shin, now able to speak without fear of being killed, piped up. "You have another son?"

Ryuu replied, "We do. He's going to be two years old soon, too."

"We named him Issey because he is our firstborn," Mikaro supplied.

"Congratulations," Horo said, bowing once more. "I bet he's the pride of your souls."

Ryuu pulled Mikaro closer, kissing him tenderly on his cheek as if he were touching his own heart, so soft and gentle and full of love. "That he is."

"And we have you, Master Horo, to thank for everything."

"What did Horo do?" Shoju questioned.

At the same time, Ryuu, Mikaro, and all the others had begun disrobing so they could join them in the waters of the sacred pool. And even from that simple activity, Shoju realised another thing.

The connection between Alpha and Omega went far beyond physical touch or knowing glances. There was a care there, as if they were both a part, an important part, of each other. One unable to function without the other, almost. Something so precious and pure, it made Shoju's heart sing to witness it.

He then wished it was so between him and Horo, even though their love was as profound as any other. Again, the desire to have his child overwhelmed him. Pity that could never happen.

Not without a miracle, anyway.

Ryuu, now naked and in the water with Mikaro sitting in front of him between his legs, both men with their hold over his distended belly, replied, "All I can remember is that after Master Fuoco took me into a private tatami room so he could decide whether or not I'd be chosen, I reacted badly to the drug they burned within the brazier. A drug I believed was supposed to subdue me so I would be more accepting as to what they had in mind."

Shoju knew that part all too well. "It relaxed me so I got sleepy." And for the first time, he understood the extent of the evil he'd been chosen for. In the end, and with not too fine a point on it, what the masters did amounted to nothing short of drugging boys so they could then sexually abuse them. And what's more, if the brazier smoke didn't work as planned, then there was the oolong tea, too—the drugged beverage that tasted like alcohol.

Ryuu clearly didn't get to drink the tea.

Horo moved to hold Shoju. "I'm so sorry, but again, I did what I had to do so as not to arouse suspicion so I could help you. I hope you understand, my heart."

"I do." And Shoju did. Shin and Itsuki, now playing the wrestling game with the other four men of the secret village, were proof of his word. Horo had acted like their master to save them. "And I love you for what you did. For all of us."

"Thank you, my heart; that means so much for you to say that."

After nods of agreement from everyone else, Ryuu continued, "And yes, it was you, Master Horo, who recognised what had happened to me when the others panicked and left me alone while I convulsed on the tatami mats."

"I did," Horo said. "I'd seen it before."

"What did you do?" Shoju asked.

"Being someone who dabbles in herbology, I gave Ryuu a tea blend I concocted that I knew would act as a sort of antidote to the drug," Horo explained. "From there, I rushed him to the rejection gate where I knew Mikaro would be waiting—as selected Omegas do each choosing season. The rest, as they say, is history."

Mikaro tilted his head now. "We are thankful you did that for Ryuu, Master Horo."

"It was love at first sight," Ryuu chimed in. "Again, we have you to thank, Master Horo."

Horo raised his hand gracefully. "Please, both of you, call me Horo. Just Horo. I'm no one's master any longer."

Shoju turned his head so he could kiss Horo's ear with his love, love he knew would never die. Not after what he'd heard. "Except for you being *my* master, of course."

His kiss was returned, that time on Shoju's mouth with a hint of his tongue covered with his saliva parting his lips. "Of course."

Light laughter resulted between them all.

Those following moments were the best in Shoju's life. Carefree and wonderful all at once. The water was so cool against the sticky heat of the day, and he loved it so much. That, and the company of his new friends, which was simply fantastic. He felt rich. Rich beyond any wealth. But most of all, it was the love Horo held for him so dear that affected Shoju the most.

Shoju whispered, "I love you, Horo," as Horo lay him down on the shore again, cradling his head to protect him while in his arms.

"I love you, too, my Shoju, my heart."

Yes, an Alpha and an Omega held a special bond, that wasn't in doubt. Shoju could see it clearly between Ryuu and Mikaro, even when they came together and kissed, both of them excited by their closeness so their erections had to be dealt with moments later. But what Shoju had with Horo, that was also something amazing.

It was the bond of a soulmate.

And after Shoju had realised that, their lovemaking on the shore before they left for the secret village, the way Horo connected with him, was better than it had ever been.

So much better.

And while Horo fucked Shoju, Ryuu took Mikaro in the same way but in a position more comfortable considering his pregnancy. Shin slid inside Itsuki as the other four men stood guard.

Those moments were peaceful and full of passion.

Shoju felt so safe and loved in his man's arms while being guarded; it was one of the most profound feelings of them all. The truth be told, he was so aroused, he came twice: once shuddering uncontrollably when Horo came inside him and again when Itsuki and Ryuu came into their respective lovers.

It was like they were all in chorus.

Shoju was certain even the birds and insects all around the pool watched in awe and silence. He couldn't blame them. It was something so beautiful that it brought tears to his eyes, which Horo kissed away tenderly.

"We must go now," one of the men said after they'd all

dressed; Shoju couldn't remember his name. "I believe we won't be alone for too long."

"What do you sense, Tora?" Ryuu asked.

That was him. Tora. The biggest of them all, muscles on top of muscles, he was. Shoju liked him because, even though he wouldn't want to cross him, as an Omega of the secret village, like Mikaro, he held a gentle softness about him, too. A protective softness that made him shine in Shoju's eyes.

He wondered if Tora had an Alpha waiting for him. Shoju hoped he did, as he hoped the others did as well. Everyone deserved love. Deserved it as strongly as he felt it for Horo, no lie.

"There are temple guards blundering around through the forest nearby," Tora explained, looking intently at the tree line. "And they make so much noise about it, even the Kami themselves could hear them from beyond Heaven's gate. If anything, by sheer dumb luck alone, they'll eventually find us if we stay here."

"Then we must go," Mikaro interjected. "Lead on, my friend."

Tora bowed. "Follow me, please. The path to the waterfall is treacherous and needs your full attention, even those who've walked it many times." He gave Ryuu and Mikaro a nod at that. "And please, do as I do, and don't wander from the path I forge. Understand?"

There was no argument.

3

Mat didn't know when darkness had fallen.

He'd been too worried about Akai to be concerned with anything else. Over the past few hours, Akai's mood had darkened as much as the skies outside the only window of the room they'd been incarcerated in. The small window barely let in a breath of air, although it certainly let in the weather.

Thankfully, it was high summer, and the night wasn't too cold.

Still, seeing Akai huddled in the corner of his cage, weeping softly, broke Mat's heart even more. He wanted to comfort his beautiful man. Be with him for the rest of his days without the hindrance of metal bars between them.

"We'll get out of here," Mat said weakly in a turnaround from before when it was Akai who'd offered the encouraging words, not him.

"I was…wrong," Akai replied with a heaving sigh. "It's hopeless."

"You weren't wrong. You were—" The door to the room opened, stopping Mat's words.

Gorou entered, again holding a tray of food and water.

The servant walked with his head hung low, as always. The two guards who'd escorted him waited by the doorway, looking unimpressed. Perhaps because they'd been given such a duty.

A lowly duty, no doubt.

When Gorou opened the slot so he could place the tray upon the ledge, Mat said, "It's nice to see you again, Gorou."

Without looking up, Gorou replied, "I remember who you are."

That was something positive. "That's good, right?" Mat came closer to the ledge, grabbing the tray. On it were two bowls of miso soup with thinly sliced vegetables sparsely floating around within their insipid-looking broths and a tall glass of water. The obvious intention was for Akai not to get a drink this meal.

If Mat's treatment as an outcast and an Alpha was harsh, Akai's as an Omega was far, far worse. That much Mat could tell already, and they hadn't been caged for a full day yet.

Before Mat could tell Gorou to give the water to Akai, the man whispered, "I can help you."

Mat wasn't sure how to proceed; whether his proposal was a set-up or a genuine offer to help, he wasn't sure. "What can you do for us?"

Gorou shook his head. "I can help you, but I won't help the other one."

Mat was taken aback. "Why not?"

"Because he's a filthy Omega, that's why."

Mat was stunned even more. "Wait…so you believe that? Truly?"

Gorou stood silently for a moment. "It's not normal, is it?"

Mat knew what Gorou meant but pressed on. "What's not normal? Two people loving each other, and through their love, they make a family together? Isn't that how you were born? Because of the love of your parents."

A snort. "I wish I wasn't born."

Mat didn't know which way to turn when it came to his conversations with Gorou. The man was scarred, and not in the physical sense, either. "I promise you, if you help *both* me and Akai, I'll help you too."

Gorou looked up. "You're a liar."

Mat opened his arms, a gesture that was meant to say "look at me" because he really needed Gorou to look at him in the cage, naked and unable to do anything, not even touch the man he loved. "I don't think I'm in a position to lie, do you?"

"All of them lie to get what they want from me." A snorting laugh that time. "Oh, Gorou, you're so handsome. Gorou, I need you. Will you do something for me, and in return I'll do something for you, Gorou?" Gorou spat on the ground by his feet after hocking it in his throat for a moment. "I've been raped more times than I can count because of their lies."

Mat's stomach turned. "I'm sorry."

"Stop apologising—you already did that."

Mat wasn't sure again. "Then what do you want me to say to you?"

Gorou came closer. "My, you're so handsome, aren't you, Matashi?"

A woozy feeling overcame Mat as he realised what was going on. "Let me guess, you want to fuck me in exchange for your help?"

Gorou smiled. "Now you understand."

Mat folded his arms after stepping back. "You've got no intention of helping me."

"I could just fuck you anyway, if that is my pleasure. You're lower in status than even me, and that's something I plan to use to my fullest advantage."

"How about you go fuck yourself, prick—do us all a favour?" Mat couldn't believe the turn of events, the sudden change in Gorou. Mat had really thought he was different. "And I genuinely felt sorry for you, too. Too bad you had to open your mouth and prove your true nature, hey?"

Gorou held his smile until one of the guards approached to tower over him. It was wiped away when the tall, muscular man said, "What's taking you so long here, *servant?*"

"I'm sorry, sir." He bowed low, holding the position for a long time. "I will be quicker next time."

The guard placed his hands on his hips. "For your slackness, I should make you get onto your knees so you can suck my cock until I shoot my load into your worthless mouth."

The bow didn't stop. "Whatever you want me to do, I desire it, sir."

"You're pathetic." The guard cuffed Gorou over his head, causing him to yelp and cower before scurrying away.

Mat wasn't sad to see him go. "And report to Master Fuoco, quick smart. Tell him of your failure here tonight. I'm sure you'll then wish you'd swallowed my cum instead of what he'll have in store for you."

No reply as Gorou ran out of the room.

The guard turned to Mat. "I'm sorry about him. He shall be replaced."

Once more, Mat didn't know what to say, only managing a quick, "Thanks," before he realised the guard was staring at him funny.

What did *he* want from Mat?

The next words the man spoke surprised Mat. "My name's Daisuko, and—" He looked around. "I was one of Master Horo's guards before he helped Shoju escape and fled to the secret village with him."

Mat could have been knocked over with a feather. "Master Horo is Shoju's caretaker?"

"That he is."

"Wait…" Everything spun as Mat's mind worked overtime to try and piece it all together. "Wait, so that means…that means Master Horo and Shoju are heading for where I'd come from before me and Akai decided to come rescue him?"

A nod and a glance at the doorway where the other guard stood. "It looks that way."

Mat felt awful. If only he'd waited an hour or so before charging off, then he wouldn't be in this mess with Akai right now. "I wish I'd known this earlier," he said to no one.

Daisuko answered anyway. "But *I* can help you."

Mat, being cautious now after his experience with

Gorou, said, "I'm not interested in your help if it means you want something sexual in return from either me or Akai."

"Or the both of you together."

Mat's heart sank. "Yeah…whatever, it ain't happening."

Daisuko creased the corner of his lips. "If I wanted you or your Omega, nothing would stop me. But no. I'm willing to help you without wanting anything in exchange other than the knowledge you'll be free."

Mat looked at him, right into eyes that seemed to reflect the shocking truth. This man really seemed to want nothing from them. Honest. But Mat wasn't sure, not one-hundred percent sure, despite seeing the conviction in Daisuko's expression.

"Why would you do that?"

"Because my brother is an Alpha to one of the kindest and most beautiful Omegas there is. And as such, I'll do anything to help my kin if I can."

"What's his name?" At that, Akai sat up, wiping his eyes, a newfound hope sparking within his brilliant blue eyes. "The Omega your brother mated with, I mean. Please tell me, Daisuko."

"Tora," Daisuko said with a longing sigh, as if the exhale of his breath was a perfect expression of his longing to see his family. It was tinged with a resigned sadness because he knew he couldn't. "The Omega's name is Tora."

Akai gasped, almost in wonder, if Mat wasn't mistaken. "Then your brother's name is Nobira, right?"

"That's right!" Daisuko confirmed. "You know him?"

"All Omegas and Alphas know each other—but Nobira

is now an elder of our village thanks to his kindness and compassion and skills as a worthy leader."

As wonderful as it was to hear such things, Mat decided to steer the conversation back on track. Otherwise, he was sure the journey down the road of nostalgia would be a long one. "How can you help us, Daisuko?"

The guard turned to him. "As I'm in a more privileged position within the temple—a captain of the guard, if you will—it's my right to take whatever prisoner I want into my bed. A perk of the job, hey?"

Mat knew where this was going. "I see." He narrowed his eyes.

Daisuko continued, "But of course, I won't do anything to you or Akai; it'll all be an act." A moment of pondering. "Although there's one problem I can see with that plan."

"What's that?" Akai asked.

"I can only take one of you." Daisuko heaved a breath. "And that means the other one will have to remain until another plan can be thought up."

"Then you take Akai," Mat said without hesitation.

Akai, his eyes still watery and red-rimmed, blurted, "I'm not going anywhere without you, my beautiful."

Daisuko pressed his lips together. "There may be another way."

"What's that?" Mat asked, curious but anxious at the same time for the answer.

"If I can get one of the other guards to agree to it, we can take both of you. One each, if you will."

"Would someone else be willing to play along with this

ruse?" Akai asked, standing now, that hope in his expression brighter despite the turn again.

"Maybe."

"You don't sound very confident, Daisuko," Mat observed.

"It's not that I'm not confident. Finding someone else will be easy." Another pause. "It's just that even though I won't touch you because you are kin…in a way…I can't guarantee the other guard won't do so to whoever he takes, of course."

Mat came closer. "Then you take Akai to your bed as arranged and let your friend take me—I can handle myself."

"I'm sure you can," Daisuko said. "But it may mean you'll have to bend over for him in the slim chance that you'll get to escape with Akai. And yes, make no mistake, this *is* a slim chance. A very slim one."

Mat's resolve steeled. "Let me worry about that. You just do your best to ensure that slim chance we both have of getting out of this hell hole isn't as slim as it could be, all right?"

Daisuko nodded. "Then tomorrow night. As far as the rest of the temple is concerned, I'll take Akai for my entertainment. I'll also have one of my friends take you. It may not be perfect, and things can go wrong, but that's the best I can do, I promise." He glanced at the doorway, somewhat nervously, if Mat wasn't mistaken. "I'll see you soon."

The guard walked away.

When Daisuko was out of earshot, Mat whispered to Akai, "Let's hope we can trust him."

"If his brother is mated to Tora, as he claims, then I'm sure we can."

"And if he's not?"

"Please don't think like that," Akai said, brightening. "We need to have *some* hope that what we were told was trustworthy if we're to get through this."

"Easy for you to say," Mat began with a sigh. "You're not the one who's probably going to get his ass pounded by some oversexed temple guard puffing and sweating behind you."

Akai offered a dismissive gesture. "I'm certain it won't come to that."

"How can you be so sure?" Mat asked, worry stabbing at him as much as his yearning to touch and hold Akai.

There was no answer.

After the tranquillity and love of his time at the sacred pool, Shoju quickly realised he was not cut out for any sort of trekking through the thick, humid forests on the leeward side of the mountains so soon.

Actually, scratch that—when would he *ever* be ready for such arduous exertion? Because quicker than what Shoju would have liked, his whole body ached, and he was tired to his bones. To add to his discomfort, sweat dripped rhythmically from his hair, and his feet were sore and blistered from being in only tabi, his geta shoes broken and discarded long ago.

Despite all that, he tried his best to keep up with Tora and the others but ultimately failed. The man led at a relentless and arduous pace as he dashed through the forest, nimble as a fox.

"I n-need…to rest for a…for a m-minute," Shoju protested, panting and feeling woefully inadequate because they'd already had a break not that long ago, and he needed another already.

The trees around him spun, he was that giddy from overexertion. Although, before Shoju could even begin spiralling about how he saw himself, his thoughts darkening about his weight most of all, Horo grabbed his hand to steady him.

Horo rubbed his thumb over Shoju's knuckles lovingly. "I'll always be here for you, my heart. Don't you worry."

Shoju melted under Horo's attention; his man clearly saw love when he looked at him. "I appreciate…t-that."

"You're so beautiful to me, Shoju, that even the most perfectly composed poetry by the grand masters of the craft couldn't begin to express the way I feel about you."

Shoju's cheeks burned as he averted his eyes. "You're just…saying t-that."

"Then let my kiss speak my truth instead."

He looked up. Horo tugged gently on his chin to bring him closer, and Shoju was soon consumed by the truth of his man's words through his touch, lips on lips, stolen breaths, all tender and caring as well as full of his love.

As promised.

As desired.

Shoju almost cried as he forgot about everything else, the lump in his throat growing. And as the world around him melted, Horo was all that mattered within the euphoria he felt all around him like a warm blanket; the worries that'd stained his thoughts before were wiped away.

The slate was now clean.

If Horo loved him unconditionally, Shoju didn't want to get down on himself because of that same love he needed to return. Sure, sometimes such things couldn't be helped, and depression gripped him often. How could it not? He was who he was. And yes, even though love healed, it couldn't change the past. It could only build the future.

Shoju and Horo's future.

When they parted, Shoju still dizzy but for a different reason, a good one, Horo said, "Take your time resting. Take all the time you need." He gestured for Shoju to sit upon a fallen log covered in mushrooms and lichen here and there in patches. "I know where Ryuu and his husband and their friends are headed. And besides, it's not far to the waterfall that acts as the gate to their world now, anyway."

As Shoju sat, relieved to be doing so, studying Horo at the same time, love in his pounding heart to fill it to overflowing, he had to ask, "Um…*their* world?"

"Yes, their world," Horo began. "The secret village is nestled within an ancient caldera and is full of nature magic. Magic the men of the secret village worship. Therefore, in thanks, the Kami who've lived there since the dawn of time have blessed them with the ability to give birth to ensure their survival. That's the legend of how the Omegas were created."

"That's amazing."

At that time, Shin and Itsuki joined them—holding hands, as always.

Shin said, "We heard there are strange beasts and all sorts of wonders there, too."

Itsuki added, "And fruits and vegetables as big as you've ever seen them, honest as I stand here."

"Hmm." Horo nodded. "All true."

"I can't wait to get there," Shoju said, feeling better now that he'd rested and hadn't been told he was a burden as he'd believed. Shoju then had a thought. "Your parents told you all this, didn't they? That's why you know so much."

"They did." Horo pecked Shoju on his still warm cheek. "I wish you could have met them." Sadness flashed in his eyes. "I would have loved to have had their blessing to marry you, my heart."

Shoju didn't know what to say to that.

Ryuu, returning from up ahead with his husband, Mikaro, said, "I didn't know we were resting so soon."

Horo stood, arms folded. "Shoju and I needed to sit down for a moment. So, we stopped."

To Shoju, the reply almost seemed defensive, but he didn't interrupt. Shin and Itsuki had backed away, clearly feeling the same tension Shoju did—the air thicker now than any humidity could create.

"Easy now." Ryuu said, diffusing the building pressure before it escalated into something Shoju didn't want to think about. "You're not a master giving orders here, Horo. Please do remember that."

Horo stared for a moment before he relaxed, offering a slight bow of his head. "You're right, of course, Ryuu. Lead on. We won't stop again. But just know, not all of us are men of the forest or have the Kami's blessing for such endeavours. *Please* consider *that* as you set your pace."

Mikaro bowed. "We also apologise, Master Horo. Tora is determined to get back to his husband, and nothing the Kami place in his path can slow his resolve. They haven't seen each other for two nights now, and the pull of the Alpha and Omega bond tugs on his heart more than anything else imaginable."

Shoju understood that. He'd pine for Horo if they were separated, and he wasn't even an Omega.

Horo asked, "What is his husband's name, my friend?"

"Nobira...why?" Mikaro replied.

Horo simply smiled, eyes glinting, as if he understood something. Something profound. But before Shoju could ask him about it, Mikaro hissed an "ahh" through his teeth while he rubbed his distended stomach.

Ryuu's concern became evident as he came to hold his husband without delay. "Are you okay, my love?"

Mikaro calmed while he continued to rub himself, obviously trying to soothe the restless baby within him. "Seems our son is trying to tell us something, because...ahh...he just tried to kick my kidney into my liver, it would seem."

Ryuu seemed to relax. "He's going to be a warrior, for sure."

"Oh, that he is." Ryuu and Mikaro kissed. "And he'll no doubt help us defend the village against the evil of the temple like you do, my husband."

"Amen to that," Ryuu said.

Shoju loved watching them, their love, the connection they had because of the family they'd made together. He then felt those pangs of jealousy once more.

He held Horo's hand, blurting without thought, "I *wish* I could have your baby, Horo. I really do." And to hear himself admit that out loud, Shoju once more burned right down to his neck.

They all looked at him.

Shoju felt the weight of their stares, terribly so. "Sorry," he said. "I-I know it's a fantasy, but it's w-what I'd like to happen…because I love Horo so much."

"And I love you, my heart," Horo interjected without delay, embracing Shoju tightly at the same time.

Ryuu then said the most surprising thing, words that almost made Shoju faint—he certainly felt giddy because of them. "Oh, but you can have Horo's son."

"Wait, what?" Shoju was stunned. "How?"

Mikaro said, "If you stay within the nature magic surrounding our village for many full cycles of the moon, then your body will be changed if you so desire it, Shoju."

"I do desire it!" Shoju felt great joy within his heart, so much so his body felt lighter and he went giddy. He wanted to get to the secret village even more now. Oh, how wonderful it would be to be loved by Horo, fucked as much as possible in the hope that one day he'd get pregnant. That he'd be an Omega. "I really do!" he added.

Horo looked stunned. "Will all of us be as affected if we remain within the secret village?"

Ryuu said, "No. If you are Shoju's Alpha, then the magic won't affect you. The Kami always provide balance. That is the way of things."

Shin and Itsuki looked excited. "We get to be a family, too, then?"

Mikaro nodded. "You can be, yes."

The news was so exciting, Shoju couldn't contain himself. "Then what are we waiting for? Let's go."

Ryuu laughed. "I take it Tora's pace won't bother you as much now, am I right?"

Horo chimed in, "It would seem that way—but, nevertheless, a slower one would be appreciated."

Mikaro, rubbing his stomach once more, nodded. "I agree."

4

The sleepless night, one full of yearning and the need to be with Akai most of all, wasn't the worst of Mat's anguish. He began to get edgy, the weight of his imprisonment pushing against him until, at times, he felt it was hard to breathe.

He hated being caged.

And what added to his plight was simply the fact he couldn't hold Akai's hand. Not even the merest touch. The cage around Mat was the cruellest thing that could have happened. He'd gone from the soaring heights of consummated love one moment to the desperate depths of forced separation the next, and Mat didn't know how long he could cope.

He hoped above all else that Daisuko's plan would work.

Mat also hoped he could trust the guy.

"I know we can trust him…to a certain extent," Akai offered, once more being hopeful and as if reading Mat's thoughts.

"I'm really trying to believe that."

Akai stood, reaching for Mat as Mat tried to reach for him. They still couldn't touch—the distance between them might as well be an ocean. He felt great sorrow as he tried once more with all his effort, stretching and aching because of it, to no avail.

Mat, hurting from his efforts, gave up. What was the use of trying, anyway? At that moment, Gorou entered the room carrying their breakfast tray. As usual, he hung his head low.

Although, this time, there was something different about him.

To Mat's concern, despite what had happened yesterday between them, the servant shuffled toward the cage with a terrible limp and a wincing sound punctuating his laboured breaths.

"What's happened to you, Gorou?" Mat asked as soon as the tray was placed upon the ledge, noting how once more there was only one glass of water.

A glass he and Akai would have to share.

Gorou looked up, distance in his stare. "How do you know my name?"

"What do you mean, how do I know your name? You told me it yesterday? Don't you remember?"

Something awoke in the man's eyes for a moment before quickly fading back into the depths from where it came, like a sinking ship with no hope of recovery. "I don't remember much about yesterday."

Mat realised that Gorou had been broken far worse than he first thought since being chosen to join the temple as a servant, but he was taken aback, nonetheless. "Err…why not?" he asked, trying not to sound too harsh but failing as he heard the question leave his mouth.

Mat would never forget the man telling him that he'd like to fuck him like he was nothing but a warm place to stick his cock.

Never.

Gorou didn't seem perturbed until he answered. "I was punished yesterday…that's all I remember." And that's when he shrunk, becoming half the man he was moments ago.

Mat then put the pieces together.

Daisuko had ordered Gorou to see Master Fuoco after yesterday's incident. "What…what did Master Fuoco do to you?"

Gorou mumbled before explaining, "He is the master of the ropes, you know. And as such, for my punishment of going above my station, he strung me up and left me there overnight after he'd stripped me naked and raped me many times." A wince. "I can't feel my left leg now."

Mat was shocked. "That monster. That fucking monster."

Gorou's shoulders heaved. "You're Matashi Soju, aren't you? You're Ryuu's brother. I used to be friends with Ryuu."

Mat's stomach tightened. "I'm Matashi, yes." He reached out to touch the man. From that contact, small as it was, Gorou's tears fell. "And if it's the last thing I do, Gorou," Mat said, "I'll come back for you and all the others like you, so you don't have to keep living in this nightmare."

"I appreciate that." He sniffled as he wiped his eyes after removing his hand from Mat's touch. "And I'm sorry."

"What are you sorry for?"

"I…don't know." More tears fell. "But whatever I did, I'm sorry."

Mat couldn't help but feel a little emotional himself. "You don't need to apologise, either. Not ever. What they've done to you…this isn't your fault."

Gorou nodded. "I'd better get going. They watch me all the time."

Mat said, "I'll see you at lunchtime, then."

There was no reply as the man shuffled away.

When alone once more, Akai said, "We've got to help all of them."

Mat knew that to his bones. "We've got to help ourselves first."

"Then let's hope Daisuko is trustworthy then, huh?"

Mat managed a smile as he looked upon his beautiful man, sunlight from the window above dappling all around him to make his nakedness glow. He was angelic. Simply stunning. Oh, by the gods, how he wished he could touch Akai one time before tonight, when Daisuko's plan was supposed to be enacted.

"Having doubts, Akai?"

"There are always those, especially in here."

"I hear that."

The rest of the day was uneventful. After all, being locked in a cage not only caused mind-numbing boredom, it was uncomfortable most of all. For a start, the straw itched everywhere, including Mat's balls, which he'd scratched and scratched, almost to the point of being red raw. But to make matters worse, the only time they saw anyone to offer any variation or stimulation was Gorou at meal times.

Not even the guards entered the room any more.

Perhaps because the place was starting to stink, seeing as Mat and Akai had no choice but to do their business in a corner, leaving it there to attract the flies.

Didn't they clean the cages?

That, however, became the least of his concerns. Because Mat noted how Gorou's limp hadn't gotten any better as time wore slowly on. Perhaps it was worse, in truth.

Mat worried about Gorou.

"I think the ropes must have cut off the circulation in his leg for too long," Akai observed, once more speaking out loud Mat's thoughts after lunch was delivered; they, as Alpha and Omega, really were connected in more ways than Mat had first believed.

"I believe you're right."

After that, Mat and Akai entertained themselves for a moment by watching each other masturbate. He wished it were Akai's hand over him, but needs must as the devil drives, as his older brother Ryuu had told him one day after catching Mat touching himself in the bathroom. It was more than embarrassing at the time—he could laugh about it now, though.

Mat missed Ryuu.

But he wanted Akai most of all.

"I'd rather have tasted yours, Akai, than me having to lick mine off my own fingers," he admitted once he'd cleaned off his stomach from the results of his efforts.

"You will soon," Akai said, bringing Mat back to the moment.

"I sure hope so." Mat shifted his weight. "Because, by the gods, I need you to fuck me so hard I'll be rendered speechless. I really do."

Akai shivered visibly, lips quivering. "Likewise."

By the time night fell, the darkened sky filled with silver-lined clouds, thanks to the moon becoming new as the month progressed. That's when Daisuko decided to grace them with his presence.

"Where have you been?" Mat had to ask, somewhat miffed, if he was being honest.

"I had plans to make," was the direct reply.

Mat didn't know what to say.

A man with a stern expression stood beside Daisuko. He was pleasant looking, tall, and built of muscles like the rest of the temple guards were. No surprises there—the thin and weaker boys were never chosen for guard duty.

"Who's that?" Akai asked, sounding as concerned as Mat was all of a sudden.

Daisuko cleared his throat, gesturing to his counterpart. "This is Botan, and he's agreed to help us."

Mat didn't know what Botan had been told, but when he spoke, that sure came into sharp focus. "Which one of them is the one I get to stick before I take them to the kyozetsu gate?"

"Um…" Mat offered, about to add more—a piece of his mind, in fact—when Daisuko interjected, "This is Matashi, and he's the one who'll go with you, Botan."

Botan's expression turned into a gut-churning leer

when the man studied Mat. "I like him. He's pretty." A lick of his lips. "He's got a pretty cock, too."

Mat swallowed hard. "So…it comes to this, hey?"

Akai said, "You promised us you'd make sure we were safe, Daisuko."

"No!" Daisuko shot him a glare. "I promised you both that I'd get you out of here, and that's what I'm doing." He held the expression, one that sent fear through to Mat's heart. "And if Matashi is required to be head down and ass up for Botan for that to happen, then so be it. Got it?"

"Then the deal's off," Akai shot back with more venom, not fazed by the man's foreboding presence. "The cost is too high. I'd rather stay in here than know my Mat has been touched by another man in the way that only I should touch him."

Daisuko snorted. "No, you wouldn't."

Mat couldn't argue with Daisuko's logic. "It's okay, Akai. I can handle it."

"But…Mat—"

"It's okay," Mat repeated to reassure his lover; his Omega; his beautiful, beautiful man. "We can't help anyone else if we're stuck in these cages, now, can we?"

Akai opened his mouth, no doubt to protest, when Daisuko interrupted, "Whatever we're going to do, we'd better hurry. The change in guard happens in an hour, and I want you both long gone before that happens."

"We've gotta go," Botan reinforced.

From there, Daisuko let Akai out of his cage, taking him away immediately without another word. While that happened, and while Mat was freed by Botan, he realised the man could do a hell of a lot of fucking in an hour.

Mat sighed, one that sounded like defeat.

Not only were his itchy balls sore from the lice-infested straw, his ass would soon be, too, no thanks to the deal they'd made to gain their freedom.

A deal Mat wasn't so sure about any longer.

But what made it worse, if at all possible, was that Mat didn't get to touch Akai as they were both snuck out of the room they'd been imprisoned in. Not even a glance at each other, really.

Mat ached to be with Akai.

And before he could consider his next move as to how he was going to make that a reality, if indeed there really was a chance of making it one, he found himself in Botan's one-room accommodation within the temple grounds.

The place was sparsely furnished: only a bed, a dresser, a chair, and a small table to be seen. It seemed the temple masters didn't want those who served them to have any luxuries.

Botan, wasting no time, touched Mat tenderly upon his cheek, an action that sent a cold shiver all through him. "You're so pretty."

"Let me guess, you want to pound my ass into next week, right?" Mat asked with a resigned sigh, mentally preparing himself for what was to follow. He had to do what he had to do to ensure his and Akai's freedom. There was no other choice. "And if you do—because, hey, why else am I here?—can you at least…you know…give me the courtesy of spitting on your cock before you stick it in me? Lube matters, you know."

Botan pulled his hand away, as if Mat's skin had burnt him.

Mat became curious. Before he could question what was going on, that's when Botan's expression changed to one of sadness, as if a different personality within him had suddenly gained dominance over the previous one.

It was both scary and captivating to watch. "What's the matter?"

Botan, with a voice that was small and weak now, replied, "I don't want to do that to you, Matashi."

"You don't?" Mat was relieved and surprised all the same, even if something had clearly happened with Botan. "Then…what do you want in exchange for helping me?"

"I want you to…" Botan's cheeks reddened, and he shifted his weight. He hung his head, too, just like Gorou did. "I would like you to hold me and tell me that I'm a good boy…please."

"Wait…what?"

Botan, in a complete turnaround, unexpectedly cried. Cried like a baby. "I used to…be the love of my p-parent's eyes, being their…only son," he blubbered, thick tears falling onto his cheeks. "But now…now it's all d-discipline, shouting…and…and p-punishment and…" The massive bulk of Botan's body shuddered with his obvious outpouring of grief, one that'd been held in for so long. "I need s-someone to tell me they're…proud of me and that they…they l-love me."

Mat, without thought, embraced the brute of a man,

holding him tightly. "You *are* a good boy, and you *are* loved."

What else could he do?

From there, Botan and Mat sat in the chair together. And even though he was still naked, not even the offer of a robe given, Mat didn't care. This man, this gentle and emotional man—now that the truth of his heart was thankfully revealed—clearly needed him.

Like all the men within the evil grip of the temple Masters needed him.

And help them all, he would.

Mat cradled Botan's big head, soothing his thick, black hair and rubbing his strong back while the man broke down and bawled his eyes out. While he shuddered and hiccupped and cried and cried. Mat had no choice but to sit with him and comfort him while he waited for the floodgates to close.

"You're such a good boy, you know that, don't you?" he cooed.

"Thank you…Papa!" Botan held Mat back with just as much intention…and love. It was a moment, truly. "Thank you. I always try and do my…b-best for you."

Mat realised the separation from his family had been Botan's biggest trauma after he'd been selected as a guard, his life from there not exactly as he'd imagined it, Mat knew.

He couldn't blame Botan for that. Mat felt the same. Since he'd left his family—a family who had no idea what had happened to him, other than that he was an outcast— there was a hole left in his heart.

Mat's anger grew when he thought about how the boys

chosen for the temple were abused, tortured, mutilated, and raped after being promised a good life.

The masters were fucking bastards, no lie!

"I know you do," Mat replied with conviction, playing along and wanting to. "And I'm proud of you for that, Botan. Really proud, my boy."

Botan's tears fell harder and faster.

After an eternity of Botan pouring out all that had to be drained from within him, he sat up to wipe his face, looking at Mat with deep relief. There was calm there, too, in those wet and red-rimmed eyes. "I'm sorry I came on all strong earlier when we were back in the cage room," he said. "But just know, it's a necessity to act tough here, and I didn't want anyone overhearing me being sympathetic. That's not tolerated, and the punishment is severe."

"I understand." And Mat did. "I get the impression every poor fucking boy chosen for temple life has to put on an act to survive." He thought of Gorou. Shoju as well. What his companion had gone through during his trials, Mat shuddered to think.

"They do." Botan got up. "Now, let me get you a spare samue, a pair of pants, and my old tabi and geta so I can get you out of here, my friend."

Mat breathed a sigh of relief. "Thank you."

"No, *thank you*!" Botan stood, offering his hand.

Mat accepted, as he'd accepted Botan. "Let's get the fuck out of here!"

With the pace slowed as promised, it was Ryuu who led them through the thick, humid forest this time. A forest that darkened quickly, Shoju noted.

Tora walked behind, guarding their rear position. From what, Shoju shuddered to think; although the noises of the approaching night soon closed in all around them, increasing his concerns. Some of the noises were frightening, like growls of hunger from beasts unnamed, or the mating calls of wolves, ferocious and frequent. Others were more pleasant, like the chirps of crickets. But it was all so new and, therefore, scary.

Even the canopy above seemed to move with a different kind of life within its branches. Always rustling, worryingly so.

"I do hope we get there soon," Shoju said to no one in particular.

"Not far now," Tora replied from behind, his voice like an apparition appearing from nowhere, like the mists that now swirled at their feet.

"Good," Horo said; to Shoju, he added, "Are you okay, my heart?"

"I am, thank you."

From there, things went smoothly, even if Tora barked a few warnings whenever they traversed trickier ground. "Watch out for that shallow ditch; it's camouflaged by undergrowth, and you'll twist an ankle if you step in it," was one such warning. There were many others, all along the same lines.

Shoju was thankful for them all, really.

Horo…perhaps not so much. "He must think we're babies who've been left in the woods without a clue as to what to expect, I'm sure."

"Aren't we?" Shin asked.

There was no reply.

Aside from his tiredness claiming him again, Shoju trudged on, even if sweat and soreness were his constant companions. The only breather he got was when Mikaro had to stop a few times to catch his breath because of the baby within him becoming active.

Ryuu always tended to his husband with love and care, their connection of Alpha and Omega plain to see even to those who wouldn't know of such things. As Shoju hadn't known only a day or so ago. He would have merely seen them as lovers. But Ryuu and Mikaro's love went deeper than that.

Their love was that of the family they'd made together.

Shoju desired that for him and Horo.

Longed for it above all else.

Which made Shoju wonder why—if being separated was so painful—the other men of this group patrolling the forests didn't have their husbands with them.

To Tora, he asked that exact question.

"It's because my husband is an elder of the village," was his direct, almost snapping, reply. "And needed at the village."

"I see." Shoju didn't really, but he let it be.

Horo, coming closer, whispered, "He needs cock up him, for sure."

Shoju giggled.

Soon, as darkness crept with more purpose through the forest, desperate now to vanquish the day, it seemed, Shoju heard the fall of water before he saw it. He quickened his pace, even though he was exhausted.

Thankfully, not only was Horo always there helping him whenever he needed it, Shin and Itsuki were, too.

Shoju would be lost without them.

When he finally saw the extent of the wonder that was the gate to the secret village within the caldera Ryuu spoke of, his breath was taken away. The towering waterfall was massive. No wonder he'd heard it from a distance: the water thundered, loud as anything. What's more, the spray added even more humidity to the already thick air.

"Come!" Ryuu ordered from the front of the group, wiping his brow. "We're almost there!"

Shoju grabbed Horo's hand. "I can't wait to see Mat again. I've missed him so much."

"If he hasn't done anything silly," Horo supplied. "Like returning to the temple after being named an outcast."

"He would only do so if he was trying to get to me."

And that was when Shoju began to worry, stomach turning. Surely Mat wouldn't return. Would he?

"As I said," Horo continued, "let's hope he's here."

5

Mat followed Botan to the kyozetsu gate, nervous as they slowly, carefully, and methodically made their way toward his freedom. Most times, he held the man's hand or grabbed his arm, but that was more out of need than anything else.

Surprisingly, Botan was his strength at the moment; Mat was relying on him more than he'd relied on anyone else in his life. A strange feeling. But if there was one thing he knew without a doubt, if there was one simple truth now laid bare, it was the fact that if he was captured again, it would certainly mean his death. The Masters of the temple didn't take too well to disobedience. He imagined they didn't take well to anything that defied them or threatened their superiority.

Not at all.

As such, to avoid being seen for fear of his life, Mat made sure to do as he was told and when he was told. Thankfully, to aid in their escape, the moonlight was obscured by thickening clouds. Perhaps a summer storm was brewing?

Mat didn't have time to contemplate such things.

The gate loomed like an opening to paradise. So close.

Yet, like all things, he wasn't out of the woods, so to speak. They still had to cross the paved courtyard. The other thing Mat worried about, which now struck him worse than his previous thoughts, was the fact that Akai and Daisuko were nowhere to be seen.

All that greeted them was the cold looming stone wall of the temple no man could climb over because of its sheer height and its smooth surface, crafted by expert artisans many centuries ago.

"They must have already gone through the gate," Mat suggested hopefully.

"Maybe," Botan replied. "Maybe not."

Along with everything else, a stab of worry found Mat. "Where could they be, then?"

Because as they approached the gate, it was clear Akai and Daisuko were nowhere to be seen. Also, the bolt was still in place within its chamber to signify the gate was locked; if they'd gone through it, the mechanism would have been slid across into the open position. Mat worried even more, so much so his stomach now tightened.

Botan shrugged. "Maybe they got caught."

Mat, not wanting his thoughts to veer down that path—not at all—shot back, "Don't say that."

"What if it's true?"

He shook his head. "I've got to believe they've been delayed."

Another shrug from Botan. "Why would you say that?" the guard asked, looking confused above everything else then.

"Because I have to think like that, that's why," Mat said

with determination striking him. He knew if anything had happened to his mate, he'd do whatever it took to get him back. "Akai *is* my Omega, and even though I don't fully understand how it all works, what with me being his Alpha and all, I know in my heart that I couldn't live without him. Probably couldn't breathe without him, either."

Botan's expression flashed a sudden change. He averted his eyes, the sadness of before coming to the surface again. "You don't know how lucky you are that you have someone who loves you."

Again, Mat understood Botan's reason for saying such a thing. Knew it all too well. He opened his arms for the big man, the intention of his gesture unmistakable. "If you need me, I'm here for you." And Mat meant it, every word.

Botan sniffled and took a heavy breath. "I'll be…all right."

Mat nodded. "The offer is always there if you need it. Just so you know that. Okay?"

"I may yet need it."

Mat sensed an underlying meaning behind what Botan said. "What are you saying?"

"I'm saying…no matter what happens, I'm coming with you." Botan looked up, his watery eyes steeled. "I can't stay here anymore where there's no love, only abuse. I don't want to, either."

Mat nodded. "I understand—but what about your family? Won't the masters punish them for your desertion? Won't they take away all the privileges they gained because you were chosen for the temple?"

Botan snorted. "The masters won't do that."

"How can you be so sure?"

"Because they'll be too embarrassed to admit to the village elders that one of their subordinates, a guard such as me no less, has dared leave the temple of his own free will. They rely on the village to provide them with chosen boys each season. That's why nothing will be said. And that's why I'm coming with you."

"That and the other reasons, I'm sure."

"Yes, Matashi, you're right." Botan offered a weak smile. "Being treated like a dog with no rewards wears painfully thin after a while. I know that all too well, I do."

"I get that." Many thoughts swirled around his head because of the change in the flow of their conversation while they waited for Akai and Daisuko—hopefully it wouldn't be a long wait, either.

The most prominent of those thoughts was that Shoju's mother would still be looked after despite him escaping with his caretaker…with Master Horo, no less.

Mat couldn't help but see the amusing side of that revelation.

The other temple masters certainly wouldn't want to admit their failure. A triple failure, really. Because not only had one of their subordinates escaped—their honoured, too, no less—so had one of their own. And that would be the ultimate embarrassment for them.

"Look! Akai and Daisuko are coming," Botan announced to Mat's profound relief, the guard's excitement clear as he pointed to the other end of the courtyard where the darkness revealed movement. "Look!"

Mat looked. His heart skipped beats as well, he was

certain. Because as soon as the clouds cleared, all he could see, all he *wanted* to see, too, was the beautiful sight of his man bathed in cool, waxing moonlight as he approached. Mat got emotional. His heart raced, his skin itched with excitement, and the yearning within him almost took his breath away. He ran to his man, his mate, his Omega, without delay. Without thought. Without care, either.

Akai ran, too.

Somewhere at the midway point between them, they met. "I was so worried about you," Mat said, his voice a quivering mess.

Akai didn't get to answer. Mat crushed him in a loving embrace, tight and needy and oh, so wonderful. To hold him. To take him in. It was amazing.

Mat could cry; he really could.

At the same time, he pressed his lips against Akai's, loving that he now could because they were no longer caged. Their contact, their love, their special bond, too, made the moment profound and strengthened their connection, if that was at all possible.

But there it was.

His heart raced even more as different urges overtook Mat. He melted. He had his soul with him once more. The other half of his world that was so dark when it was absent, even for a flickering moment, had returned.

Not being in Akai's arms, near him so kisses could be stolen at any moment, was like being eclipsed by something terrible. A monster clawing at him. Darker than darkness, really, because it pierced him to his soul, staining it with its emptiness.

And Mat didn't want to feel like that ever again.

No wonder he felt so complete because Akai was with him again. And as such, his kiss, longing and passionate, lasted a brief but perfect eternity, one long enough to convey his feelings but at the same time short enough for them to get on with what that had to do: go through the rejection gate to gain their freedom.

Be together forever without hindrance.

When they parted, a string of their drool hanging between them until broken by the increasing distance, Akai, breathing hard and his voice heavy with as much lust and love as Mat felt, said, "We had to stop for someone."

Mat licked his lips, loving the taste of Akai upon them. "Who the hell did you stop for? I was worried—" It was then Mat understood, his words taken from him as it dawned on him, the reason for Akai's delay. Sure, he couldn't believe his eyes at first, but he was also thankful Akai and Daisuko had brought him along. "I'm glad you could join us, Gorou."

And Mat was, truly.

After all, it wasn't Gorou's fault he had behaved the way he had. It was the masters of the temple who'd broken him, who'd tortured and raped him until his only defence was to hide within himself or lash out like a cornered animal.

Mat took Gorou's hand.

At the gesture, Gorou smiled but looked bewildered at him. "Who are you?"

Mat simply replied, "I'm a friend."

Botan placed his hand on Gorou's shoulder. "Let me

look after you, Gorou. I think you and me understand each other, am I right?"

To Mat's surprise, instead of holding his smile, Gorou looked shocked and shrunk under Botan's attention. "Are you going to rape me now, guard?"

"No, no. Not at all." Botan, equally shocked, grabbed Gorou's hand, the one Mat held. "I'm going to look after you from now on. I promise."

Gorou's lip quivered as he stared at Botan for the longest time. "You mean that?" he finally asked, his voice croaky and breaking in parts as something came over him. What that was, Mat wasn't sure, but he suspected it was relief.

"I do." Botan took his other hand, bringing him close.

Gorou then did the only thing he could, Mat imagined. He began to cry, softly, but with tears that shed so much more than how he'd been treated since being chosen by the temple masters. "I don't…know your n-name, though."

Botan wept, too, as they embraced once Mat let Gorou go. "It's Botan, my dear friend. Just…Botan."

To his delight, Mat realised that two broken souls had found each other. And that was a beautiful thing. Truly beautiful. Mat could also see they had a need, a want no one else but themselves could help them with.

"You did well," Mat said to Akai.

"I know."

Botan and Gorou held each other for a while as they let their emotions flow. A release that could only be shared by those who'd experienced something terrible together, as they had. They understood each other, and that was something profound, for sure.

Gorou, his head resting on Botan's massive chest while his tears flowed, shuddering, sucking in breaths, whispered, "I may…forget y-your name, just so…you know."

Botan sniffled but didn't wipe away the emotions streaming down his face to drip off his chiselled chin. "Then I'll always be here to remind you, Gorou."

"I'd like that," Gorou replied. "But I can't walk very well anymore."

"I'll carry you if I have to."

"Thank you."

Mat hoped they'd also begun the long road to their healing, confident the journey had begun in earnest. He turned to Akai, feeling the need to hold him now. "Are you crying, too?"

"I can't help it." Akai wiped his eyes.

"Come here and give me a hug, my beautiful and sexy soft boy."

Akai let Mat pull him closer, folding himself into Mat's arms. "There's a part of me that isn't so soft, for your information."

Mat looked him in the eyes, the blue of them still dazzling even under the gloomy moonlight obscured by clouds. "When we're in the safety of the village, you can get that part of you into me once you've spanked me hard, all right?"

"I can't wait."

Mat was about to say he couldn't either when Daisuko

interjected, "I've opened the gate, so please, let's not waste any more time. Go, my friends. Go!"

Mat realised something else. "You're not coming with us, Daisuko?"

Daisuko shook his head. "No. I'll better serve our goal by remaining here. Just know, I'll keep doing my best to help those who need to escape the temple. That much I promise, Matashi."

"You're a good man, Daisuko," Akai said. "A good man."

Daisuko patted Mat's and Akai's backs in turn. "Just spend your days making beautiful sons together, so that one day there'll be more men to oppose the evil of the temple."

Mat said, "One day fucking soon, hopefully."

Botan and Gorou were already through the gate, the guard helping the servant walk by supporting him around his waist with his strong, muscular arm. It was a lovely sight. Although, as soon as they disappeared into the darkness beyond, a bell tolled.

Mat gasped.

Daisuko warned, "Quick, there's no more time! The alarm has been raised, and you must go now…*please!*"

Mat didn't need to be told twice.

Hand in hand with Akai, together they ran into the misty forest, their goal the secret village. But first, they needed to avoid any guards who might follow them beyond the shadow of the temple.

That would be their first challenge.

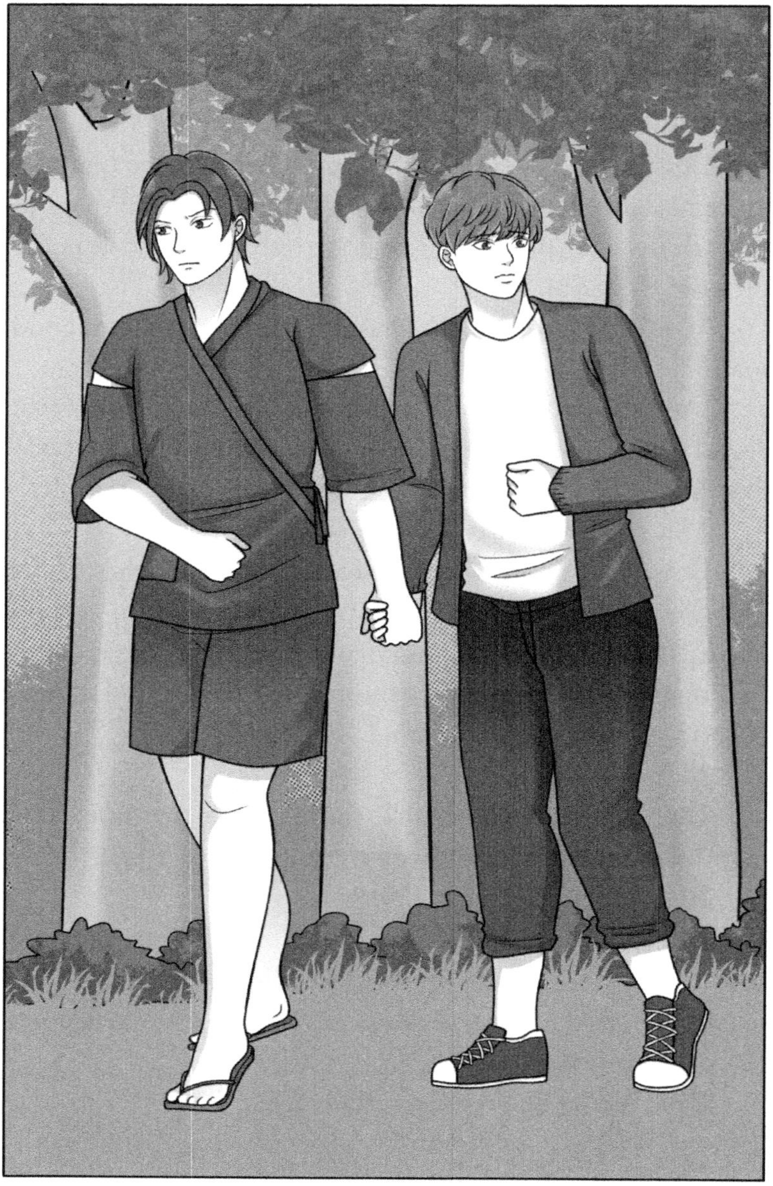

Shoju soon found himself within a land he couldn't believe, not even in his wildest dreams. Many times, he had to hold on to Horo. The world within the caldera was indeed magical—beyond belief, really.

He was left dumbfounded, because even if the shroud of night obscured a lot of the wondrous landscape before him, enough of it was revealed by breaking clouds to be blessed by the moonlight. The sight was something special to behold.

Shoju began, "This is…" He couldn't finish his words, he was that awestruck, his mouth dropping open as he came to stand in front of a mushroom as big as he was; a caterpillar the size of his arm, shoulder to wrist, crawled lazily over its cap.

"…Unbelievable," Horo finished for Shoju, adding what seemed like a contented sigh. "And I have to tell you, I feel like I'm truly standing on the soil where I belong."

"That's because you're home." Shoju pulled Horo closer, holding him tightly. "This is where your parents lived, and as such, this is where we'll live, too. I can feel we both belong here. I can."

"We *do* belong here."

Shoju kissed Horo's cheek before moving to face him, slipping his arms around his man's waist. "Here is also where we'll start our family, if what the others have said is true about the magic of the Kami blessing me because I desire to be your Omega."

"As I desire to be your Alpha above all else, my heart."

Horo and Shoju shared a kiss, one bathed in moonlight and full of their passion. Their connection, sensual and needed, declared before the Kami of this place, really, meant that something strange overtook him. Something Shoju couldn't quite understand himself because it hadn't happened before. It was a deep feeling. A connection to Horo he knew went beyond what he already had.

He also felt electricity course all through him: not the wonder of close contact to create the sensation of such, but the feeling of an actual spark. One that caused his skin to ripple with gooseflesh. To describe it, Shoju could only say magic had shot through him.

Magic caused by his love of Horo in this place.

Horo only nodded. He then stood silently for a moment, looking around, breathing deeply as he took everything in. He truly looked happy, the joy on his face clear.

Clear to Shoju, anyway, because, again, there was that deeper understanding of him. As if Horo's emotions had become more focused so he could read them better, even the subtle nuances of them.

Absolutely wondrous!

Although, before Shoju could add anything more, explain his thoughts to himself or soak in the wonder around him, Tora yelled, "Nobira! It's so good to finally see you!"

Tora ran ahead of the arriving group to greet his

husband and mate. Both men quickly flew into each other's arms, folding themselves within each other's love after that. It was a wonderful sight, the bond between them needing no other explanation. They just were.

"I missed you so much, Tora. So, so much!" Nobira said, the hunger and yearning in his voice unmistakable.

"As I missed you, my universe."

They kept holding each other, kissing deeply, as if they were all that mattered. As if no one was watching. Like they, within their own world that they now shared once more, most certainly were alone.

Shoju knew it to his bones.

Because that's how he felt about Horo. His love went so deep for him that to even be parted from his man for a moment would be an eternal pain. A torment, really. The electricity continued to ripple through him in ever-increasing waves.

Shoju realised Horo felt the same, more so when he said, "My cock aches for you as much as my heart."

"I think…no, *I know* I need you to fuck me right now." And it was true, the urges overtook Shoju unlike at any other time.

He'd not felt like that before.

Sure, he desired Horo. Wanted him inside him often. But this new sensation? It was completely different. To Shoju, it was like Horo's physical love was something he now couldn't live without. Not at all. Horo's love was like the air, life-giving and profound. Shoju shuddered, breathing harder the more he held onto Horo.

He was completely infatuated to the point of blindness.

"I feel my need for you, Horo, and it's consuming me like a fire," he moaned, knowing he was sweating from his passion, his saliva filling his mouth as much as he leaked pre-cum into his fundoshi.

Shoju's thoughts were on nothing other than Horo and his love. Well, that wasn't entirely true. He thought of Horo's throbbing cock most of all because he needed it deep inside him.

He told Horo as such, his voice breathless.

During Shoju's fall into the depths of his desires, Ryuu came over to them. When that happened, he wasn't sure. Shoju was too concerned with other matters.

The matters of his heart.

Ryuu said, "I can see your bond must have already been strong for you to both feel the pull of the nature magic so quickly. You're truly Alpha and Omega, Shoju and Horo. Truly meant for each other, and you are welcome here. Most welcome."

"What does it mean for us, though?" Shoju asked with a moan and shudder while Horo's touch on him intensified, the electricity shooting through him even more to further engorge his growing erection.

Shoju ached to the point of pain.

Ryuu offered a knowing smile. And even though Shoju couldn't focus—the man looking blurry within his vision all because of the erotic haze Horo's closeness brought with it—he heard in reply, "You know what it means."

And suddenly, Shoju did know.

He moaned again, opening his mouth for Horo, his drool dribbling onto his chin. "I want you to mate with me," he begged, not fully understanding why he'd chosen those words but loving the fact that he had.

Horo didn't seem taken aback; in fact, he was more than willing to comply—to Shoju's delight. "Then let me lay you down."

Ryuu chimed in, "You must go to the Moon Room where all Alphas like to mate once their Omegas come into heat."

Come into heat? Shoju didn't understand what Ryuu meant, but he could certainly feel it: the deep desire within him to be completed by something other than the sum of his own parts. The miracle of the nature magic coming to the fore, if he was to quantify it. Which he couldn't, really. All he understood, all he accepted, too, was the urge increasing to have another within him. To have Horo within him.

His desire to have a baby.

To have Horo's son.

It was almost intimidating, if he was being honest. He felt as though he'd opened up completely as he became more and more soaked in his own needs and in the magic of this place, which seemed to prickle at his skin. Shoju's mind, as well as his body, was now willing to accept what would follow.

To accept the gift of life given to him through his love.

Shoju felt elated by that revelation. "Because of what this strange magic has done to me already, from now on when you cum in me, Horo, there's every chance I'll become pregnant."

"Then let's not waste any more time," Horo replied hungrily, the fire in his eyes reflecting how Shoju felt.

More shudders as Shoju warmed further. More moans, too, as the "heat" Ryuu spoke of grew as much as his lust for Horo did. His cock hardened even more, aching right down to his balls. But most of all, there was an even greater love between them, one he hadn't experienced before.

Ryuu quickly led them to the Moon Room.

Shoju was becoming desperate, and he began disrobing along the way. By the time they arrived, he was down to his uncomfortable fundoshi. The door was opened for him, then closed once he entered with Horo. Shoju didn't care what the room looked like, only that it had a comfortable place for him to lie down. It did. The futon-style mattress upon the tatami matting was soft and billowing.

It was perfect.

The room also had a window above so that the moon of the room's namesake could be seen when it made itself known through the clouds. The knowledge that it was coming to its fullness drove Shoju into an even greater frenzy; drove his desires further.

No sooner had Shoju been placed on the bed where he'd be loved than Horo ran his hand over Shoju's stomach, his touch delicately edging lower toward his erection. "Does it turn you on knowing that when I fuck you, I'll also be putting my baby into you as well, my heart?"

"It's my every desire to have your baby, Horo. So, yes, it turns me on like nothing else."

"I can see that." Horo tugged down the cloth of Shoju's fundoshi, grabbing his cock tightly. "I can feel it as well."

Shoju trembled. "Give me more than you've ever given me, Horo."

"More?"

"Yes, more! I want you to spit on my face and body as much as you do into my mouth when we're close. I want to feel you wet me, leave me dripping as much as you'll leave my ass dripping. I want to drown in your love as you give me what I desire."

"That's…that's so sexy," Horo said, his voice trembling.

"Then *please* get on with it."

Shoju, losing patience, pulled Horo up so he'd stop playing with his cock—dilly-dallying, really—clawing at him, raking his nails over his back. The hunger he felt made him shudder and writhe underneath his man, and he loved it.

Shoju growled.

A moment later, they were kissing, deep and sucking and full of their spit. Horo parted many times to do as Shoju wished, hocking so that he could drench Shoju in his fluids.

"Oh, yes!" Shoju said, elated, quivering, grabbing again, and moaning, as he felt Horo's saliva drip off his nose, eyebrows, and hair. "Give me more while you fuck me, *please*!"

Horo shuffled into position, using his drool to slick his hand. From there, he lubricated his thick, hard cock. "I'll give you whatever you need, my heart."

"Treat me like you own me; keep spitting on me to mark me as yours while you're inside me."

"Perhaps I should spit all over your ass as well to ensure you are truly marked!"

"Oh, god, yes!" Shoju arched his back in yearning, his cock as hard as he'd ever felt it. He was leaking so much, his pre-cum a thick, clear dribble. "Spit all over me, then cum inside me, please, please, please." He was so hot now, it was almost unbearable. "I so want that, Horo."

"Then that is what you shall have."

Horo leaned over Shoju, drooling once more into Shoju's open, willing mouth. He loved the taste of his man, tangy and sweet at the same time. More so when it was dribbled right onto his tongue.

He closed his eyes, waiting for what was to follow, opening his legs more for Horo. At first, nothing. Then, as Horo continued to drool onto his face and into his mouth—so good—Shoju felt him move lower. The unmistakable sensation of his man's warm saliva dripped off his balls, cock, and hole.

But Shoju wanted more because he knew he was close to climax.

So close.

"Yes, Horo!" Shoju moaned more and more as Horo attended to him with more purpose, and he suddenly felt himself let go, his release like an explosion after so much tension had been built up. "Keep marking me as yours." He shuddered as he came and came, every muscle in his body taut as he blew all over himself, his cum mingling with Horo's drool.

Shoju collapsed, panting, sweating, dripping wet with Horo's efforts and his own, skin glistening, but the desires within him didn't recede. How could they? The dance of their love wasn't done yet.

"I'm going to fuck you now," Horo announced. "I'm so turned on; I really can't describe it."

Shoju felt himself harden even more, his balls tightening already. "You never need to ask permission, Horo. Fuck me whenever you desire it. Do what you want to me, too. I'm yours. Always."

"Thank you, it's appreciated." Then, his movements full of intense heat and passion, Horo entered Shoju without further delay, lifting his legs to do so.

The penetration, the moment of truth as it were, was full of blissful pain. Agonising and wonderful.

So goddamned good.

Shoju yelped but quickly encouraged Horo to keep going. He also opened his mouth again, tongue lolling and ready to be dominated as much as the rest of him. Horo's eyes ignited. He really was the man Shoju loved with everything he had, and right now, Horo was all he could see.

All Shoju cared about, too.

Horo's thrusts were carnal and wild, sinking into Shoju right to the root of his cock. More shudders. More writhing with joy. More heaving breaths as they became one.

As they connected unlike any other time before.

Not only was Shoju filled more than enough because of his man's excitement—his own arousal growing, too—but he realised with everything he had within him that he needed Horo's cum to impregnate him. Only then would his satisfaction be complete.

Shoju grabbed at Horo once more, spurring him on with more moans and his feverish actions, hands all over him. He wrapped his legs around Horo as they pressed their lips together. They kissed deeply and with sucking wet lips, groaning, trembling, their tongues fucking each other's mouths as much as Horo fucked Shoju with his throbbing, thrusting cock.

Shoju wanted the moment to last forever.

To his growing delight, it almost did, because Horo wasn't done. Not by a long shot. He was clearly aroused, far more than he'd ever been because of what they were sharing this time. The bond they had, heightened to unbelievable heights thanks to the nature magic all around them.

Soon, Horo gained his rhythm, sweat already dripping off him to add to all the other fluids Shoju was covered in.

This was better than even his deepest desires.

Shoju was in heaven.

As Horo fucked and fucked, Shoju was slammed against the bed with even greater purpose as his man's thrusting gained in intensity. "Ah! Ah! Ah!" he blurted with each pounding push. Shoju was going to be sore, but he didn't care.

Not at all.

He loved that he was being fucked roughly, almost without care. Like Horo was an animal needing to mate. Because, in truth, that's what this was now. A mating.

Horo was truly breeding Shoju.

"Oh, yes!" Shoju said with joy, Horo still deep inside him. "That's it! Fuck me harder! As hard as you can."

Horo grabbed him around his hips, moving him where he was needed to please Horo. Thrown all over the bed, really. Actually, he was pulled off the bed and fucked while bent over. Then they were on the floor, Horo shoving Shoju onto his back, his stomach, and on all fours. Shoju let the man do as he wanted.

Shoju loved it.

So much so, he squirted more cum from his pulsing cock, hands free, even more than his first orgasm. It came from a deeper place within him, too, one that kept the fires burning. Shoju was drenching wet, from his own sweat as well as Horo's—his saliva, too. And that time, the thick, sticky ribbons of his release splattered all over the tatami matting because he was half-bent over, half-kneeling when he came.

Horo moved Shoju again, grabbing him and picking him up to do so. That time, he was put into a position where Shoju had to ride Horo's cock, facing him while it was his turn to lie on the bed.

"Cum again for me!" Horo ordered. "I can feel your ass tighten when you do, and I want more, my heart."

"Yes, Horo."

Shoju grabbed his hardness as he sat himself down onto Horo's cock, his legs on either side of his man. He hissed, loving the sensations of being entered while pleasuring himself at the same time, even though he was sensitive thanks to the two earlier orgasms. If he was being honest, he was so sensitive it almost hurt, especially the knob of his cock, still free from his pulled back foreskin. But he didn't want to disappoint his man.

Horo moved his hips so he could fuck in that position, grunting, sweating, shouting, too, as Shoju moved to help him. The noises and heat between them were incredible, even more so when Shoju was picked up and thrown back onto the bed, flat on his back now only to be pierced again. He loved being his man's fuck boy; he really did.

It turned him on so much.

Shoju came again, shuddering in disbelief. He hissed and quivered, the orgasm making him see stars.

Shoju almost lost consciousness.

That time, thankfully, Horo came, too. And that's when Shoju knew something was different about that. He gasped, feeling his eyes well with tears at the realisation.

Horo had collapsed over him, kissing him tenderly, pantingly thanking him, Shoju returning it in kind. But Shoju was overwhelmed, and his eyes grew wide as he felt the change grow within him. "Oh…my god!"

"What…what is it, my…heart?" Horo huffed with clear exhaustion, sweat glistening. Their marathon fuck had utilised every inch of the Moon Room, not just the bed.

"You did it."

Horo gazed deeply into Shoju's eyes. "Did what?" He paused, the elation of lust sated, replaced by a dawning realisation. "You mean…really? That soon?"

Shoju nodded, feeling tears of complete and utter joy, his desires fulfilled, his heart complete and so full of love. All that and more flowed from him like a swollen river had burst its banks. "We're…we're going to be a family, Horo. You and me. A family. Isn't it…isn't that wonderful?"

"It is more than I could ever ask for!" Horo exclaimed.

They held each other, weeping softy from their love and from the revelation of what had happened. It felt like blissful eternity passed before the dawning of a new day shone down from the window above them.

6

Mat and Akai led the way through the dark forest…well, Akai mostly did. He knew where he was going, after all. Even at night, when moonlight struggled to break through the canopy and it was difficult to see, Akai didn't seem to miss a step.

He was a marvel.

Mat thought they had to travel northward down to the leeward side of the mountain, but he wasn't too sure, if he was being honest. He'd only been to the secret village once before.

It was a place he missed because of the memories it already held—the love he'd shared with Akai most of all. Theirs was a love he needed more and more with each passing moment. The urges within were almost unbearable.

Akai's touch—holding his hand, being close to him, taking in his manly scent, feeling his warmth—was overwhelmingly beautiful. And it ensured Mat's cock remained an aching, leaking semi-erection. It had been that way since they'd left the temple. Mat's balls had quickly become tender within the confines of his fundoshi, and he had to adjust himself often to try and remain as comfortable as he could.

He'd need to find release soon.

"All these trees look the same," Mat said with a sigh, the urges within him dredging up his frustrations, too. Although he noticed the murky, mist-shrouded surroundings had lightened. Perhaps dawn approached. How long had they been walking?

"Trees are like that," Akai said lightly.

Mat wanted Akai even more now, his man's voice driving him wild. "I got that." Gulping, his cock went from semi to fully erect in the blink of an eye. He shifted his weight, moaning.

Much to his chagrin, he knew they had to press on; their safety was far more important than him getting laid right now. Mat wished they were there already. Why weren't they there yet?

All during their trek, over smooth ground or treacherous, Akai hadn't let Mat go. Not once. Not even to relieve himself behind a large tree covered in moss, something Mat admitted he liked watching. Liked it even more when Akai pulled back his foreskin just enough to make his stream flow farther, splashing on the bark proper instead of at his feet.

With the glimpse of Akai's knob such a delightful sight, Mat's urges boiled over, unable to hold on anymore, his stomach doing that whole lovely flipping thing. "I can get on my knees for you, just so you know," Mat offered. "I'd love to clean you with my mouth after you've done your business."

Akai kept his cock out. "Then do so. I won't stop you."

Mat wasn't taken aback, but he was certainly pleasantly surprised by his mate's words. "Will you fuck me, too, once I've got you hard?"

"I will, for it's what I want as well."

"Good." Mat smiled. "Because after being separated from you for a day, I know to my bones that I need you more than ever."

"As I yearn for you every moment, waking or sleeping."

But Mat had a worrying thought. "What about Botan and Gorou? I mean, I *want* you, Akai. I want you like nothing else. But I don't want to be with you if there's a chance that they'll see us together. I *don't* want that. What we have is for us, and us alone."

"You're right," Akai agreed. "Our love isn't an entertainment."

"Then…" Mat gulped again. "Then we'll have to wait until we get to the secret village, won't we?"

Sadness coated Akai's words, an emotion Mat knew all too well. "We will."

Mat and Akai, hand in hand after he'd helped his man with his fundoshi, somewhat reluctantly came out of their hiding place to face Botan and Gorou.

A good thing Mat held onto those urges of his, much to his yearning ache, because Botan and Gorou never wandered far. And even though Botan looked after Gorou, ensuring he didn't stumble—often carrying him when required, a beautiful thing to witness—the guard himself also needed looking after.

Mat and Akai would provide it, always.

He also believed Botan and Gorou were developing feelings for one another as all four of them grew to be friends. And why wouldn't they fall in love? Healing together would be a good catalyst for a romance. Then again, it could also be the water that doused their passions.

Either way, nature would take its course.

"Why do you care for me so much?" Gorou asked Botan, pain finding him as he shifted his weight onto his damaged leg for a moment as soon as they'd all set off again.

Mat worried. He believed Gorou's leg was injured beyond healing, no thanks to Master Fuoco hanging the poor man from the ceiling all night after he'd tied him up as punishment. Punishment for a minor indiscretion, really. Gorou certainly didn't deserve such treatment.

No one did.

Botan, unfazed, replied, "Because we all deserve someone to care for us, and I'm the one who's going to care for you from now on, as I promised."

"Who will care for you, then?" was Gorou's next confused question.

Botan smiled. "If you want the job, then you've got it, my friend."

Gorou blinked. A long moment passed, as if he was trying to work something out. That, or he was trying to find a lost part of himself. "I'd like to do that."

"Then that's what we'll do—look after each other, hey?"

"Can you tell me your name again," Gorou added, lowering his head. "I know you told me, but I've…forgotten it already."

Botan pulled Gorou into an embrace. "It's all right. My name's Botan, and I'm your friend. You're safe with me."

"I'm your friend, too, right?"

Mat couldn't help but think that was perhaps as far as they were going to progress now. It seemed Gorou was too broken. The evil masters of the temple really had affected him too much with what they'd done. The fucking bastards.

"I'm sorry," Mat couldn't help but blurt as his thoughts and worries swirled within him.

Botan and Gorou looked at him. "Why are you sorry?" Botan asked.

There was a spark of light within Gorou's eyes. "You saved us, Matashi. You should never apologise to us."

"All right, then." Mat held some hope for the man. For Botan, too.

Akai coughed into his free hand politely. "We must go. I don't know if the guards followed us, but I fear they have. The alarm was raised, after all."

Mat agreed. "How long until we get to the Omega's village?" Mat didn't want to call it a "secret" one any longer—to him it was secret no more.

"The name of our village is Osumase," Akai offered. "It means the end."

"The end of what?" Gorou asked, blinking.

Akai smiled. "The end of oppression by the temple and the main village of the island that supports them, of course."

"Jussei village," Botan corrected. "Seeing as we're naming things."

"Indeed." Akai chuckled.

Mat then heard the click of a twig not too far away. He

turned on his heels, facing where the sound had come from, heart pounding, throat tightening.

With his heart skipping a beat, Mat instinctively pulled Akai close to protect him. Although, no amount of protection he could give his Omega would amount to much. He had no weapon.

Botan grabbed Gorou, also for protection.

Luckily, Botan was armed.

He drew his katana, the metal hissing as it was freed from its scabbard. "Show yourself, he who dares approach us," he ordered, slipping into his guard role without so much as a blink. "And as a fair warning to you, I *will* defend my friends and my companion to my last breath."

Mat was glad Botan was with them.

Gorou seemed to appreciate Botan as well; he held onto the big man's free arm with more purpose. And if Mat wasn't mistaken, there was love in his eyes as Gorou looked up at his protector…his companion, as Botan had said.

Although, he didn't have time to appreciate their blossoming relationship—or any of his other thoughts for that matter—because at that moment, two men came crashing through the undergrowth, screaming something incoherent, spittle flying, while brandishing their rudimentary weapons high. Clubs if Mat wasn't mistaken.

"Fuck!" Mat's heart stopped skipping beats and started pounding hard against the back of his ribs. *Shit! Shit! Shit!* These two men meant business, all red-faced and unhappy to have been disturbed.

Who were they? One thing was clear in the confusion that followed: they weren't guards of the temple.

And confusion it was.

Because with a burst of power only rigid training could achieve, Botan charged forward. "I gave you your warning, and you chose to ignore it! Now you'll suffer the consequences, thieves!"

Thieves?

Mat then realised who these two men were. It was obvious from their dark clothing and the dirt all over them, even on their faces. They obviously wanted to blend into the surrounds of the forest, no doubt because they were poachers trespassing on temple land. The fatted deer that lived in these parts were worth more than their weight in gold. Those caught hunting them were punished severely. Probably put to death, Mat mused.

But Mat didn't have time to consider anyone's fate, including his own. The clash of steel rang out to echo through the forest, scaring him. He'd never been in a situation like this, his nerves shredding his earlier bravado, replacing it with concern.

Mat and Akai backed away together.

It was then he saw that Gorou was frightened out of his mind, kneeling on the leaf-littered ground, holding his head in his hands while he rocked back and forth, mumbling something unintelligible. No doubt as a coping mechanism, one where he'd sort of "left" himself because of the terrible situation they found themselves in.

A situation Mat wished he could leave as well.

He felt deeply for Gorou, unable to do anything else but comfort him as best he could despite the danger all around them. And even though the poachers weren't skilled when compared to Botan, sharpened steel still cut, no matter the hand that wielded it.

A wayward swipe could be the end of either one of them.

Once again, Mat was glad he was with Akai. It took until the initial shock had worn off, but Mat realised that the two men must be known to his Omega. Akai's look of terror was slowly turning to recognition.

Akai stepped forward. "Stop! Kento—Saburo! Stop, please. We're all friends here. Can't you see that?"

The two poachers Akai had named Kento and Saburo, Mat not knowing which was which, shot glances Akai's way, then turned and ran back into the forest, quick as frightened rabbits.

Mat's nerves calmed. "What was *that* all about?" He couldn't believe his eyes, even though he'd witnessed it.

Akai shrugged. Unfortunately, before he could add words to his gesture, it was clear that Botan—all balls and bravado in equal measure—must still have been fired up from the fight, from steel against steel. He gave chase, the big man screaming a war cry as he disappeared into the darkness between the trees, hellbent on finding the two men.

Silence then.

Mat couldn't help but see the amusing side of all this. The situation had gone from a dangerous one to a ridiculous one in a split second.

But, still, he had to do something. "Stay here with Gorou, Akai. I'll go get our overenthusiastic warrior before he hurts someone!"

At that moment, adding more "what the fuck?" to the whole turn of events, four more men appeared to confront Mat, Akai, and Gorou. Great! Mat could shoot this whole day down, he really could.

Were Kento and Saburo merely the diversion? The gang of poachers using the tactic after years of experience, no doubt. Seeing they were now outnumbered; Mat raised his arms. "I give up."

Yet again, it was good Akai was with them. His man simply smiled, opening his arms. "It's good to see you, Tora and Nobira. You as well, Mikaro and Ryuu. Very good to…"

Mat didn't hear any more. He was stunned to the point of being frozen on the spot. What did Akai say? Had he heard him correctly? Okay, the four men weren't poachers. Obviously not. No, they were Omegas from the village of Osumase come to greet them. And not only that, one of them was…who? Did Akai say Ryuu? As in his older brother, Ryuu?

What the hell! How could that be?

It was impossible, right?

Through the gloom, Ryuu came to Mat, smiling nervously, and he opened his arms as much as Mat's heart had opened when he'd recognised his brother. "It's been a long time, brother. Too long."

Without thought, Mat fell into his older brother's embrace, feeling more at home than he'd ever felt in his life. He couldn't help it; he got all emotional. "I-I thought…you w-were dead."

"As you can see, rumours of my demise have been greatly exaggerated."

"I'm so p-pleased right now, honest as I stand here."

Ryuu gently pulled himself out of Mat's hug, ending it far too soon. "This here is my husband, Mikaro," he said, gesturing to a handsome man, dark-haired and tall.

"He's…pregnant," Mat blurted, not wanting to sound rude, far from it. He was pleased by the news. Pleased beyond anything for so many things, really—the main one, of course, being that Ryuu was alive!

Mat wiped tears of joy from his eyes.

Not only did he have Akai—forever his Omega, his love, his man—by his side, he also had good friends in Botan and Gorou. And now he had Ryuu back, too. His brother was alive! Absolutely unbelievable! Wow! Mat was elated. He still couldn't grasp it all.

What a night!

Tora, a massively muscled man, all stern looks, cloudy expression, and an imposing presence, interjected, "There'll be time for family catch-up when we go retrieve your friend before he kills those poor poachers."

"I have so much to tell you, Matashi." Ryuu always used Mat's full name. He didn't mind that, not one bit.

In fact, Mat realised he'd missed hearing it from him. "I have much to tell you, too," he blurted, his mind spinning now with everything coming to the fore.

"I know." Ryuu glanced at Akai, a smile crawling over his lips. "It seems my husband isn't the only one with a son in him, is he?"

"You…you can tell just from looking?" Mat was again

astonished. "I only mated with Akai recently, and I know he doesn't have a sign above his head…does he?"

Ryuu laughed, as did Akai, who then explained, "The bond between Alpha and Omega that you now know so well, my love, is also a bond between all Omegas. We all know when we've mated, when we've given birth, even when we've found our Alpha."

"That's amazing," Mat said.

Nobira chimed in, "No, the nature magic of the Kami is amazing." But at that, he looked down at Gorou, who was still huddled on the ground. "This one is broken, and I don't need magic to tell me so."

Mat replied, "Gorou needs our help, no doubt about it."

Akai said, "He's been treated terribly by the temple masters. I fear the circulation of his left leg has been cut off for so long it'll go gangrenous if it's not tended to soon."

Nobira clicked his tongue. Tora approached, as if an unspoken communication between them had summoned him to his side. They held hands for a moment, visibly relieved by the contact. "Can you please go and get the guard who gave chase to the poachers while I make sure our friends are escorted to Osumase safely? I fear these woods are crawling with evil temple filth."

"I don't want to leave you for too long," Tora protested.

"You won't."

They kissed, deep and long, before Tora did as he was asked, disappearing into the gloom with Ryuu—after Ryuu had given Mikaro a parting kiss full of love and longing as well, of course.

Watching them, Mat once again became aware of his own predicament. He held Akai's hand, the renewed connection after briefly being broken engorged his cock to aching again. The bond between them was clear and true.

It was also magnificent.

Mat uttered, "As soon as we get to the village, I'm going to lie down for you, Akai. That much I promise."

Before Akai could add his thoughts, Mikaro said, "You're the Alpha, though, Matashi. How can you—?"

Akai, bowing, interrupted, "Mat isn't an ordinary Alpha. As your husband is no ordinary Osumase villager, either, because of the way he protects us all instead of choosing to sit idly by and wait for a miracle."

A look passed between them, then Mikaro shrugged. "You're right, my husband is our protector." A smile. "But just know, the Moon Room is occupied at the moment. You'll have to find another place to consummate your love this new day."

"This late into the Moon's phases?" Akai raised his brows in surprise. "Who is it that mates so late?"

"Our newest arrivals," Nobira said somewhat proudly. "Shoju and one of our returned sons, Horo."

"Shoju!" Mat cried, his heart pleased that Shoju was safe. And settling in nicely from the sound of it.

"Yes," Mikaro confirmed. "And because their bond of love was so strong, so pure too, the nature magic blessed Shoju with the ability to bear a son already."

"My goodness." Akai gasped. "That's never happened with anyone so soon. Not that I'm aware of, anyway."

"So…Shoju's pregnant, then?" Mat was ecstatic now,

unable to contain himself. He *really* wanted to see his companion.

"He is," Nobira confirmed. "We have all celebrated this news, that's for sure. The more of us there are, the better chance we'll have against the imposing rule of the temple."

"Then what are we waiting for?" Mat said. "Let's go!"

"Unfortunately, the news isn't all good," Mikaro interjected, his words throwing a wet blanket over Mat's eagerness momentarily.

"What do you mean?" Mat asked.

Akai looked as concerned as Mat felt.

Mikaro said, "The reason we were out here in the forest before dawn was to confirm the information we'd received through our network of many sympathisers and spies."

"A network that includes the poachers your temple guard friend chased after, I might add," Nobira said, his tone darkening. "I hope he returns soon and doesn't hurt those men. They are allies."

Mat then looked down at Gorou. No change there. "Then please tell us this information so we all know." From the graveness he'd gathered from his new friends, he wished Ryuu were here now. His big brother provided him with support he realised he needed.

As Ryuu had clearly been doing for the whole village, he realised proudly.

He wanted Botan to return as well, mostly because Mat knew he'd be the only one to bring Gorou back from wherever he'd gone to protect himself. The only one who would be able to carry him, too, their bond was that strong already.

Alas, as far as Ryuu and Botan making an appearance, it wasn't meant to be. Not for the moment, anyway. Seemed Botan had chased Kento and Saburo deep into the dark forest.

Nobira, his voice wavering in an attempt to hide his concern, replied, "The temple not only stirs because of your escape this night, but the masters have set their dogs upon *us*, too."

Mat looked between them all, waiting for more.

It was Mikaro who provided it. "As far as we know, more than fifty well-armed guards are combing through the forest as we speak. They're not only searching for you and Akai, they're also hunting us."

"How can you be so sure?" Akai asked.

Nobira spoke next, the two men seeming to take turns replying. "We know now that they're heading for the waterfall gate."

Mat's heart skipped in that all too familiar way. "Then we mustn't delay. We've got to get to the village to defend it if need be."

"We're not warriors," Mikaro said. "And a lot of us are in no condition to fight, even if we wanted to." He rubbed his swollen stomach to emphasise his words.

"We may not have a choice," Mat replied. "The survival of all of us depends on us needing to do *something*, right?" He looked at Akai. "You must have weapons, surely?"

Akai squeezed his hand. "We do have weapons, yes."

Nobira supplied, "What use is steel if a lot of us don't know how to wield it?"

"Or if some of us can't," Mikaro added.

Akai said, "We have greater weapons than metal fashioned to points, might I remind you?"

Both men looked taken aback. "Are you suggesting what I think you're suggesting, Akai?" Nobira said, mouth agape.

"I am, elder Nobira," Akai confirmed with a bow. "I am."

"Then we must truly hurry, as Matashi suggested," Mikaro added.

Horo held Shoju until dawn broke. He didn't sleep. He couldn't. Too much love flowed through his veins. He was also too excited, wondering what his son would look like now that Shoju was pregnant and he could think such wonderful thoughts.

"I'm truly blessed now that the love Horo gave me grows inside me," Shoju whispered to himself. He rubbed the place just above his pubes in little circles, a warmth spreading through him as he imagined how he'd been blessed with a womb because of the Kami of this place. Because of his bond with Horo, as well.

Shoju was at peace.

Horo stirred beside him just then, but that wasn't what disturbed his serenity. Outside, there seemed to be a commotion going on. Shoju sat up, concern crashing through him as the voices outside became louder.

Horo woke proper. "What's the matter, my heart?"

Before Shoju could answer, there was a knock on the Moon Room's door. Shoju didn't move to cover himself. Now that he was fulfilled—loved and in love—he didn't feel the same about his body; he now loved his curves and extra padding, mostly because he felt so complete for the first time in his life.

"Enter," Horo said as he got up, slipping on his robe.

Within a blink, Matashi burst into the room. He was holding a strikingly handsome man's hand. It was clear to Shoju that they had a bond. No, wait. He knew without understanding how he knew that the man was an Omega, and he had within him Mat's son.

Mat was an Alpha!

Shoju jumped up off the futon, crushing Mat into an embrace, one full of his love for his companion of so many years. "About time you got here! I was so worried about you when I heard last night that you'd gone to rescue me."

"You have Akai to thank for that."

"Thank you, Akai." Shoju smiled as he brought Mat's Omega into the hug as well, feeling Akai's arms fold around them. "And I'm glad I didn't have to go get you myself, Mat."

"The worries aren't over," Akai announced when they'd parted.

"What do you speak of?" Horo chimed in, placing a robe over Shoju's shoulders and tying the belt for him after he'd slipped into it.

"War is upon us," Akai said dramatically.

"War?" Shoju repeated, his insides tightening.

Horo grabbed Shoju's trembling hand. "What's the plan?"

"As the village elder, Nobira has called a meeting to discuss it," Mat explained. "And if we don't hurry, we'll be late."

Shoju feared what was coming. He worried for everyone in the village, but his thoughts were on Horo and their son most of all, if he was being honest. He felt as if the years he and his man could spend loving one another and raising their family were at risk of being taken from him. And because of that, he'd do anything he could to prevent such a thing from happening.

Anything!

7

The whole village had gathered, more than five hundred men with worried expressions. There were also a couple of dozen boys of varying ages, too, from toddlers to late teens—every one of them sons of their proud Alpha and Omega parents.

A few of the men carried babies. A few more were in various stages of pregnancy, from being close to term as Mikaro was, to only recently being blessed, as Akai and Shoju had been.

"You know, there aren't as many boys as I thought there'd be here," Mat said. "Considering how many men there are."

"Alpha and Omega pairings aren't as common as we'd like them to be," Akai said stoically. "I only got to be yours because I was chosen to go to the rejection gate this season, and fate played her hand in our favour."

But Mat had a question, a different curiosity burning. "Are all of the boys born here Omegas?"

"They won't be until they reach puberty; and even then, they have to remain within the village until that time." Mat shot him a questioning glance. Akai added, chuckling, "But to answer you, because I know that look, Horo isn't an Omega, even though he's the son of an Alpha and Omega couple, because he wasn't born here nor did he live within the nature magic while he grew up. He wasn't able to develop his womb."

"Ah." Questions swirled in Mat's head while Nobira began the meeting by announcing for calm. In a lower voice, Mat said, "But Horo turned out to be an Alpha, though, didn't he?"

"Because of Shoju," Akai replied quickly.

"Why did I become your Alpha, then?"

"Because of me."

Mat believed he understood. "So, the Omega is the one who chooses his Alpha? That's why couplings aren't as common, as you say. Because the Omegas of Osumase have to go out and search for their Alpha. Is that it?"

Akai squeezed Mat's hand. "Something like that…but it's also a little more complicated. There has to be that connection, too. That spark."

"I see." Mat nodded, believing he did.

But he also worried even more at the moment as a new thought struck him. Because one thing became apparent as he looked around. Very apparent. More than ninety percent of those gathered weren't ready to fight against a trained army—he could see the fear in their eyes.

The men of Osumase were peaceful.

Only the likes of Ryuu, Tora, and a handful of others seemed to have even bothered to learn the art of attack and defence. Or, at least, Mat assumed so as they held their swords properly, as far as he could tell.

At least Botan and Gorou had joined them. The two poachers had, too. They were allies, after all, and any help, no matter how small, was a godsend right about now, Mat knew.

Nobira raised his hands again. "Welcome brothers," he began. "I'm sure I don't need to tell you why we're here. We all know. What I'm here to discuss is what we're going to do about it."

Botan stepped forward without being asked. "Whatever you decide to do, it would be best to rescue as many as you can from the temple while the majority of the masters' guards approach the waterfall gate."

A rumble of voices washed through the crowd.

Nobira gained control quickly, waving his hands to settle everyone down as he replied, "That's our plan. We will split into two groups; one will go to the temple, and the other will defend our village." He paused as stunned silence took over. "Any questions?"

Mat, not understanding why, said to the gathered, "I'll defend the village with whoever wants to join me! We must protect what we have here! We must!"

Horo chimed in, "And I will lead the charge against the temple, for I know the secret places within its walls well."

Shoju grabbed Horo around his arm, protectively. "I'm coming with you."

Horo shot Shoju a concerned look. "But you're pregnant…and I don't want anything to happen to you, my heart."

"That may be so," Shoju said proudly. "But I'm not leaving you, no matter what. And besides, I may be pregnant, but I'm not incapacitated. I want to help so our son will grow up only knowing peace. I want that most of all—as I'm sure everyone else here does."

There was no argument from Horo after that.

Not from anyone.

It seemed Shoju's conviction and his clear love for Horo and the family they would have stirred the feelings of the others. Roused them to action, too. Because not only did they voice their agreement, but most of them also voluntarily split into the two groups Nobira had asked for. And it was no small ask.

Not only would they be protecting Osumase, but also bringing about the downfall of the temple as well.

Mat could certainly see the change in Shoju, and he liked it. He had gone from someone who was shy and obedient without question to a man who held more confidence about him, which was refreshing to witness. He knew now he didn't have to worry about his companion any longer.

Shoju could look after himself.

Akai, bringing Mat back from his reverie, said, "You may not even have to get too close to the fighting, either. Not for those who don't desire it, anyway."

"What do you mean?" Mat asked, his curiosity piqued.

Akai smiled. "We have a way to…stay out of the way, so to speak."

Nobira smiled, too. "If I'm understanding you correctly, Akai, I believe you're talking about the large flightless beetle that lives here. Am I right?"

"You are, elder Nobira," Akai agreed, bowing. He then

explained his plan to Mat. "It's a species of bombardier, and it produces a secretion. We can harvest that, and when ignited, it's a far more effective weapon than mere steel."

A ripple of excitement coursed through the crowd; a wave of hope as well, if Mat wasn't mistaken. But for him to hear Nobira say "large," the insect must be truly monstrous. And it was all thanks to the nature magic within the caldera making everything bigger than normal.

Akai further explained, "For those of you who don't want to wield a katana or pull a bow, we have a chemical weapon at our disposal."

"How volatile is this secretion?" Horo asked. "And how much can we get in the short time we have?"

Mat knew Horo was referring to the temple guards closing in on the waterfall gate. He was sure they would breech it and enter the caldera well before the day was done.

Nobira said matter-of-factly, "It can melt metal."

Tora, moving to hold his husband, said, "Word has it the enemy is already at the river the waterfall drains into."

Mat sucked in a breath. "*Already?*"

Mikaro replied, "They have our destruction driving them. Because to them we're nothing, even less worthy than the dogs they train to sniff us out."

Shoju asked, "How did they find us so quickly?"

Horo, with an exasperated sigh, answered, "I've long suspected Daisuko as a man who plays both sides for his own benefit."

It was then Botan piped up. "The bastard. He planned this all along!"

Gorou, using Botan as his support because his left leg

was bound in bandages, the scent of exotic healing herbs surrounding him, looked confused, his brow furrowing. "But Daisuko helped us…didn't he?"

Mat, putting the pieces together, interjected, "More like he had guards follow us after the alarm was raised."

"Knowing temple tactics," Botan explained, "he would have used scouts to let the approaching garrison know where we went."

Akai spat. "That's how we were discovered."

Mat said, "Seems that way."

Nobira puffed up his chest. "Then we've got to do what we must. I'll take whoever wants to go with me to the grove where the bombardier beetles live. The rest of you, ready yourselves! We march out within the hour to confront our foes!"

A cheer rang out.

Ryuu, his katana held high, shouted, "For Osumase!"

"For all of us!" Tora added with just as much enthusiasm.

More cheering resulted. It was amazing to witness, and Mat couldn't help but get caught up in the moment. "For our sons, too!" he yelled.

When the two groups dispersed, looking to their respective leaders for guidance, Shoju cleared his throat. "Err…I'm no good with a weapon, but I'll come with you, Nobira."

"Me, too," Horo bowed to the elder. "Even though I'm trained with the sword, I'll accompany you, my heart. I'll then gladly lead the charge against the temple."

"You just can't live without me," Shoju teased, pinching Horo's arm.

Horo blushed.

Mat said, "After we've collected the beetle's secretions, we'll be ready to kick some temple ass, for sure!"

All agreed.

As Mat was about to follow Nobira and the others joining him, Akai pulled him closer. "After the enemy has been driven away, I think we'll need to attend to other matters, don't you?"

"If we had the time, I'd get you to fuck my brains out right now."

Akai sighed longingly. "If we had the time, I'd be happy to ensure your brains were indeed fucked right out."

Mat laughed, but that yearning pull within him came to the fore once more, his erection not far behind. "Then we'd better defeat the enemy quickly, right?"

"Indeed."

At that moment, Botan and Gorou walked past, the guard still supporting his injured companion. They were following Nobira, as were a lot of men now.

Mat, already sensing the change in Shoju, also got the same feeling from Botan and Gorou. But for them, it wasn't about confidence or anything else. It was about love shared because of their hardship—something pure and honest, Mat knew. "Botan and Gorou are more than friends, don't you think, Akai?"

Akai smiled. "They'll soon be Alpha and Omega, for their love is strong, and the nature magic has already begun blessing them."

Mat had to ask, "Botan'll be the Alpha, right?"

"You may be surprised."

"Wait…but Gorou…he's had his balls stolen from him, being a temple servant, and all. Right? How could he be an Alpha?"

"If gifting a man with a womb so he can bear a son is in the power of the nature magic here, surely replacing a couple of testicles is well within their abilities, don't you think?"

Before Mat could contemplate Akai's words, Shoju and Horo, along with Ryuu, Tora, Itsuki, and Shin, approached, the two poachers—Kento and Saburo—right behind them.

Ryuu clapped Mat upon his back. "Ready, brother?"

"As I'll ever be."

"Good." Ryuu glanced down. "Because all of our erections will need seeing to before this day is done."

Shoju said, "Umm…there's only one Moon Room, though…isn't there?"

Nobira laughed, grabbing Tora's hand, winking. "When Omegas and Alphas celebrate a great achievement, the billions of stars above become the ceiling, not wood or tiles—once the younger ones are put to bed, of course."

"Oh…" Mat wasn't sure about being fucked with others around him…well, not strangers, anyway. Then again, nothing was achieved yet, victory or otherwise. He'd worry about such things later.

If there was a later…

The grove of the bombardier beetles wasn't far away. To Shoju's shock, the insects weren't large at all—they were gargantuan. As big as him, if not more.

"How…how do we get at the secretion again?" he asked, even though Nobira had explained it…many times.

Horo kissed Shoju on his cheek while a particularly large bombardier beetle scurried past without care. "It takes two men, my heart. One to hold the blanket over the front of the beetle and another to palpate the secretion tube below its abdomen."

"It's the role of the one who has to do the palpating that I'm worried about. What if the beetle…you know…doesn't like being touched there?"

Mat chuckled. "Hey, you're basically going to be jerking it off…and who doesn't like that?"

Akai gave a knowing smile.

"Grab that one there," Nobira said, far more practical about things. "Tora and I will give you a demonstration so you'll know what to do."

Within the blink of an eye, Tora pounced on the beetle closest to them before Shoju could move, covering it with one of the towels Itsuki and Shin were given the responsibility of handing out. They were also in charge of the pails, too.

From there, Nobira knelt down while the bug wriggled

and squealed, which was a strange high-pitched sound, one that could hurt ears if sustained for too long. Nobira quickly began milking it like one would a cow, only in this case there weren't any teats, just a rigid tube.

Shoju winced as the stink of the secretion, gluggy and orange-coloured, oozed into the bucket Nobira held in place.

"You've seen how it's done," Nobira said. "Now get to it. We don't have much time."

A sense of urgency took over.

Shoju didn't recall how it all happened, but before he knew it, his pail was filled with the stinking, volatile fluid of the giant bombardier beetles that lived within the wonder of the caldera. From there, the secretion was transferred into hand-sized ceramic jars, perfect for throwing.

Horo took his hand. "If you're ready, we must march to the temple. But know this: I'll protect you with the last breath I have within me, my heart. I promise it."

Shoju appreciated the sentiment. "What if it's me who has to protect you, my love?" Because what he'd said was the truth to his soul. He would die for Horo. That wasn't in doubt.

Horo shot him a curious glance. "I have no doubt that you will if I need it."

"I'm glad you think like that."

"With love, is there any other way?"

After Shoju said his goodbyes to Matashi—kissing him upon his lips like they always used to—he embraced Akai and all his other friends who weren't joining his group.

Shin and Itsuki joined them, as always. As expected,

really, considering they owed Horo their lives…and their balls. Not that Horo would have looked at it that way, Shoju knew. Still, the two men would have felt compelled to do so out of duty and friendship.

Shoju was fine with that.

But to his surprise, Nobira and Tora came with them. It seemed Ryuu, Botan, and Gorou would go with Mat and Akai.

They all wished each other well.

Shoju couldn't help but get the feeling something terrible was about to happen. Aside from the inevitable conflict, that was. No. This feeling went deeper.

He feared for them all.

But he feared for Horo and their unborn son most of all.

8

The thundering of the waterfall gate grew louder. On the other side, Mat knew a garrison of temple guards approached. They were probably already there.

"What's the plan?" he asked Ryuu, his anxiety peaking for the tenth time since they'd left Osumase proper.

"When we pass through the gate, the archers will fire lit secretion-soaked arrows into the enemy's leading ranks. From there, we should be able to handle any who dare come forward."

Akai looked worried. "What if we can't?"

Ryuu said, "Then we'd better pray to the Kami of the caldera for a miracle, my friend."

Mat didn't like that option. It relied too much on misplaced hopes, as far as he believed, anyway. "What about if we use the land to our advantage? You know, be smarter, not stronger."

"What are you suggesting, brother?" Ryuu asked, unsheathing his katana, the sound of his action a comforting one. "Because if you have an idea which could give us any advantage, no matter how slight, I'm all ears."

Mat wasn't too sure, but he spoke his thoughts,

anyway. "Why don't I lead a few of us up there, where the waterfall cascades over the cliff face?" He pointed to where he wanted their attention drawn. "We can throw the jars we've filled with beetle secretion onto the enemy once the wicks are lit, right? Sort of like bombing them. That'll be an advantage to us, I know it."

"It will be," Ryuu agreed, rubbing his blond-bearded chin, the action causing a rasping sound.

Mat took that as both permission and acceptance. "Then Akai, Kento, and Saburo, you're with me. Let's go!"

Ryuu said, "Good luck."

"You, too."

Before Mat set off, he heard his brother call over Botan and Gorou with a quick gesture. Words were exchanged. Nods, too. What they discussed Mat couldn't hear, but as soon as they were done, the guard and servant headed back toward Osumase.

Did Ryuu think Gorou too much of a liability?

Mat didn't have time to ask, even though he thought anyone who wanted to defend their home, no matter their ability or condition, should be able to do so.

"We must go," Akai prompted.

Akai was right. Mat and the rest of them had to do their part to help Ryuu do his with all the other men, about one hundred or so in total. Mat could ask his brother later why Botan and Gorou were sent away.

The climb up to the crest of the waterfall wasn't easy. Many times, they all had to help each other, the rock face often precarious. Mat wished they'd been better prepared. Even a length of rope would have been helpful, for sure.

When they finally arrived, breathing hard and thankful to be at the top, Mat mistakenly peered over the edge. They were high, very high, and aside from the dizzying sensation of vertigo gripping him so that Akai had to hold him, one thing was clear.

The battle had begun.

It was a terrifying sight, one that chilled Mat beyond his bones to touch his soul. He shivered. There were many more tower guards thirsting for their blood, yelling, swords held high, than he'd been led to believe. Or did they just look like a hell of a lot of them now that he'd witnessed it?

Akai kept holding him as the haunting sound of many, many arrows whistling as they were loosed was heard above the roar of the waterfall, thick, greasy smoke lines trailing behind them.

"It's started," Akai announced.

Kento and Saburo, carrying packs upon their backs full of the volatile jars, volunteering to do so because they were used to carrying the weight of slaughtered deer through the forest, approached.

To Mat, it looked like the climb hadn't even broken a sweat on their brow. They were amazing. Fit, too.

"We mustn't delay our attack," Kento said, slipping off the pack to delve into it, handing a jar to Saburo.

"I've got the striking box to light the wicks," Saburo said. "I'll get each one ready so you and Akai can throw them without delay, Matashi-san."

Mat nodded. "Good idea."

Saburo, after receiving the first jar, struck the match

and lit the wick as he'd said he would. He handed it to Mat. "May it find its target true."

Mat smiled. He turned, moving so he could throw the jar as far as he could with all of his might. "That's for Gorou and everyone else whose lives you fucked up, you bastards."

And as the arrows kept flying, Mat and Akai hurled jars full of beetle secretion, one after the other. To see them explode in massive balls of flames and smoke, right into the ranks of the tower guards, was a beautiful sight.

The confusion it caused was the most priceless thing of all to witness.

"Give me another," Akai said.

Mat had been given one as well. That time, they both threw the jars into the bedlam below. Saburo and Kento worked hard, doing their best to retrieve the jar, light the wick, then hand one to either Mat or Akai.

They had a good system going; that was until Mat heard, "There they are!" from an angry voice that seemed too close for comfort.

Mat spun on his heels to see two temple guards approaching, their attitude glinting as much as their swords.

The other guard barked, "Let's throw them off the cliff, hey? That'll teach the filthy bastards for thinking they can take us on."

After a three-hour march through the steaming forest, Shoju dripping with sweat he wished Horo would lick off him, especially the beads trickling down from the small of his back into the crevice of his buttocks, they arrived at the looming wall of the temple. Shoju was exhausted, nervous, and elated all at once.

But for the first time in memory, he didn't feel inadequate.

"Are you all right, my heart?" Horo asked when they stopped to drink from canteens and catch their breaths.

"I'm fine, my love," he said. And he was. He really was.

There were almost fifty men with them, including the village elders, Nobira and Tora. Shin and Itsuki joined them, looking grateful for the rest. If Shoju wasn't mistaken, Itsuki looked more so. Something had changed with him. Tora approached before Shoju could ask his friend about it.

"Seeing as you know the temple grounds well, Horo, what's the plan here?" he asked with conviction, placing the two large packs he'd been carrying without complaint all the way through the forest onto the ground; the packs were full of jars containing the beetle secretion. How he managed it, Shoju couldn't guess. They must have weighed a tonne.

Horo glanced at the wall, a wicked smile crawling over his lips. "We burn the place to the ground."

"I like that plan." Tora also smiled.

Nobira said, "Then let's not waste any more time and get on with it." He gestured for the others to gather around. "The enemy approaching the waterfall gate wouldn't give us such a courtesy by waiting."

Tora gave out the jars evenly, which worked out to two per person.

Horo pulled Shoju close, kissing him on his forehead, his eyes full of tenderness and something else.

"You're worried about me, aren't you?"

"I am, my heart." After that, he handed Shoju one of his many daggers, his fingers brushing over Shoju's, sending tingles of delight through him. "Please use this if things get desperate."

Shoju accepted the blade and scabbard, securing it to his belt. "You do know I've got no clue when it comes to using a weapon, don't you?"

Horo kissed him gently on his lips that time, the worry still there. "The pointy end goes into the enemy."

Shoju rolled his eyes. "I know that bit."

"Then also know, when you use a dagger, get up close and personal," he suggested, grabbing Shoju around his waist, kissing his neck, and moving his hands lower. "Then, when you have the enemy where you want him…" Horo mimicked a stabbing action into Shoju's stomach. "Stick it into his guts quick as you can. From there, you move the blade around so you can slice open as many internal organs as possible before they die. Get up to the heart, if you can."

Shoju was overcome, feeling giddy and weak in the knees. "I appreciate the demonstration, Horo. But you've failed."

"Oh, how so?"

Shoju turned within Horo's hold to face him, lips brushing lips. "I've now got a boner, and the only stabbing I want to happen is your thick cock thrusting into my ass."

Horo planted another kiss on Shoju's lips, warm and tender. "That comes later, I promise."

"I know." Shoju pulled himself out of his man's hold, sighing. "For now, we've got a job to do."

"We do."

After their moment, Shoju settled enough to regain his resolve. He thought about all the poor boys at the temple, forced into servitude. "We've got to rescue those who need rescuing."

"I knew you'd say that." Horo moved away to draw his katana. "I'll go to the servant's quarters and do just that. I'll try and save as many as I can from castration, too."

"What did you want me to do?" Shoju wanted to go with Horo, but knew they had to split up to get more done while the others did their thing.

"I want you to find the new honoured."

"The...wait, what?"

"Once they knew you'd been taken, they would have chosen another. He needs to be freed, too."

Shoju narrowed his eyes. "Then that's what I'll do." He knew the honoured were drugged and then sexually abused in one of the many tatami rooms; he just had to find the right one as soon as he could.

Nobira gave the signal, a raise of his hand and a call for victory. From there, the rejection gate was breeched, and the flames began. Shoju wanted nothing more than to see the temple as a smouldering pile of ash upon the mountain top.

Mat stood in front of Akai, blocking him from their enemies. "Come any closer, and you'll be the ones over the cliff, not us."

The two guards didn't heed Mat's warning. Why would they? They believed they held the advantage here.

And they'd be correct.

"Or would you prefer being burnt to a cinder!" Saburo threw a jar after he lit the wick, only to have it deflected by the flat edge of the first guard's sword, the container's spiralling wake of smoke all that could be seen as it disappeared beyond sight over the edge.

"You're gonna have to do better than that," the first guard said with a grating laugh, moving closer.

"A lot better," the other chimed in, laughing just as hard.

"Then it's steel against steel, isn't it?" Akai drew his katana, its blade catching the sunlight, glinting, even though Mat could see his nervousness despite his brave words.

Akai was outnumbered.

Mat didn't know what to do, being without a weapon. All Mat knew, and to every fibre of his being, was that he had to protect Akai, Saburo, and Kento.

"Fuck!" he cursed himself as he desperately looked around.

Then he saw it. He picked up the pack containing the remaining jars, throwing it at the second guard after lighting one of the wicks.

It was a beautiful sight.

The second guard, distracted by the first guard's advance toward Akai, didn't have time to avoid the burning pack. It struck him hard, flames igniting instantly.

The second guard screamed blue murder as he caught fire. He flailed his arms around, dropping his katana as he tried to no avail to douse the flames consuming him thanks to the volatile, sticky, thick goo exploding all over him after the impact.

Mat rushed forward, seizing the opportunity he'd been blessed with because of his quick thinking. He slammed his body into the guard, sending him hurtling over the edge.

The man's horrified cry faded away as he plummeted to his death, silenced by either the flames or the impact.

Mat didn't care which; at least the man was dead.

"Good riddance, you fucker!" Mat spat, patting out a part of his robe that'd caught fire thanks to his momentary contact with the doomed guard.

But that now left them without any means of defence or attack. There were no more jars to throw down onto the enemy below. Then again, he'd done what he had to in the moment.

Unfortunately, what he'd done wasn't enough.

"Matashi!" Akai screamed, that one word chilling Mat to his soul.

He turned, only to be faced with the shocking sight of Akai on the ground, clutching his bleeding upper arm, his face a mask of pain. Kento and Saburo were backing away from the guard, who'd decided Akai was no longer a threat. The two men being were herded toward the edge, clearly scared out of their minds as they held each other.

Mat saw red.

For Akai being wounded, and for his new friends being threatened. No one, not a soul, dared hurt those he cared about. Fuck them! Again, and without thought, he picked up the dropped sword of the second guard mid dash.

As quickly as his legs could carry him, Mat charged like he was possessed, the weapon held high. His sprint was only stopped by the back of the guard once Mat thrust the blade into him to its hilt, blood oozing everywhere.

The guard didn't even get a chance to shout out in pain, the force of Mat's attack enough to pierce his heart clean through from behind. Instant death.

Fucking wonderful.

Mat spat again. "That's for hurting my Akai, you prick."

Kento and Saburo rushed to roll the body over the edge. And as Mat looked down at the sword, dripping blood onto the ground, he then realised what he'd done. A strange sensation overcame him.

He'd not killed anyone before. Now he'd murdered two men without so much as a thought.

What had he become?

It was Akai who brought him back from those worrisome thoughts. "You did what you had to do," he said softly, easing Mat's churning concerns, but also reading his mind thanks to their bond, he believed.

"You're right, I did," Mat agreed. "When I saw you were hurt—wait, let me look at that. You may need the help of a healer."

Akai giggled, waving dismissively. "I'll be fine, I know it. I have my Alpha protecting me, after all."

Mat pulled Akai into a deeper embrace, kissing him on his beautiful, tender lips. "Your Alpha needs his Omega's cock after all that's happened."

"Killing got you horny, huh?" Akai teased.

Mat thought about that for a moment. "Sometimes I really don't like you, Akai, you know that?" he also teased.

They both laughed.

"Fine with me." Akai kissed Mat once more, a kiss that lingered to arouse him even more. "I'll just stick my cock in you and dislike it as much as you dislike me from now on, okay?"

"And how often would this fucking we both dislike happen?"

"As often as you desire it."

Mat and Akai shared more kisses, gaining in passion with each passing moment. "I fucking love you, Akai, you wonderful, beautiful man. Just know that, most of all."

"I love you, too, my Matashi. My Alpha…my husband to be."

Mat pulled away for a moment. "Husband?"

Kento, disturbing their moment, interjected, "It looks like we won! The enemy is dispersing."

Mat looked over the edge. It was true. The temple guards who hadn't been burnt, shot with arrows, or killed by Ryuu and his band of protectors were fleeing, like the cockroaches scattering from the light they were.

A fantastic sight.

Against the odds, they'd won! Such a great feeling, for sure.

But Mat quickly returned his attention to Akai. "I'd love to marry you, Akai. I couldn't think of anything I'd rather do, if I'm being honest."

Akai, his eyes welling with his emotions, said, "I think it's time we re-joined the others."

"I agree," Mat replied, noticing for the first time Kento and Saburo held hands as he grabbed Akai's. At the same time, Mat couldn't wait to tell everyone their good news. He was going to be a father *and* a husband! Wow!

Inside the temple grounds—vast and pristine and a place where monsters lived despite its serenity—there was little resistance to their assault. Well, none that Horo, Tora, and a few of the other men skilled with the sword couldn't handle, anyway.

Once the last of the guards defending the temple was sent to his knees, hands bound, Shoju said, "I'll go find the new honoured now."

"Be careful, my heart." Horo sheathed his katana.

He gave Horo a parting kiss, saliva mingling to form a

bridge between them for a moment before being broken. "I'll make sure of it."

With that, Shoju determinedly headed toward the tatami rooms beyond the chōzuya, his goal clear to him. Although, the sight of the fountain's water trickling onto the smooth stones that he'd heard would be used to replace the balls of the servants who were to be castrated sent a shiver all through him. He hoped that hadn't already happened for this season's chosen boys. Still, he had no time to worry about such things.

He had a job to do.

His search through the tatami rooms proved fruitless until he came to the fourth, the smoke of destruction already finding his nostrils.

Shoju entered.

The sight confronting him took his very breath. "Master Fuoco!" was all he could utter when he'd gathered himself.

The man turned to face Shoju. He was naked, glistening with sweat and blushing from his exertion from his cheeks to his chest. The most obvious thing about him, though, was his still semi-erect cock dribbling cum in a thick thread, which dripped to his feet.

Shoju knew why.

On the tatami matting, panting and exhausted, there was a young man bound with rope using the art of shibari to immobilise him, legs held open by the bindings, so there was no doubt what Master Fuoco had done to him. His reddened, freshly fucked hole leaked cum as much as his abuser's did.

"I see you couldn't stay away from me, Shoju." Master Fuoco opened his arms. "Get down on your knees so you can clean my cock with your mouth. Then, when you've got me hard again, perhaps I'll fuck you until I forgive you for deserting us."

Shoju realised Master Fuoco had no idea what was going on outside the walls of the tatami room because he'd been occupied with breaking in the new honoured. "You're right, I couldn't stay away," he said, playing along.

A leering smile before Master Fuoco snarled hungrily. "You desire my cock, don't you, boy?"

"I do."

"That's because you're as weak as water," Master Fuoco spat, his cock already hardening, the dorsal vein bugling to make it look uglier. "That was why you were chosen as our honoured. You're obedient and weak and easy to manipulate. Now come. Do as I have asked of you."

"You're right, I am weak." Shoju slumped his shoulders as he kept up his act. "And it would be my absolute pleasure to once more give myself to you in all ways, Master Fuoco."

"Now that's what I want to hear."

Shoju stepped forward. "Can I give you a hug first?"

A visible shiver of delight. "You may, my boy. You may."

And even though Shoju was repulsed by his closeness, the stink of the man's sex and evil in equal measure, he moved so he could do as he'd said. As soon as he was in position, he reached with his hand so he could grab the dagger Horo had given him.

134   Kon Blacke

In a heartbeat, Shoju thrust it into Master Fuoco's stomach with all his might, holding him firm with his other arm so the man wouldn't be able to back away. For once, Shoju's weight was an advantage against the thin man who was more worried about where his cock went than anything else.

"What…have you…?" Master Fuoco shuddered and let out a rattling gasp as Shoju moved the dagger upward to slice neatly through his internal organs, just as Horo had told him to do.

As he did so, satisfied he could feel the life ebb away from Master Fuoco with every passing second, he whispered into the man's ear, "You forgot about how water, even though weak, can eventually break rocks. And even though you claim it's as weak as me, when you least expect it, you'll be swept away by the wave! It's my honour to be that wave, Master Fuoco."

Shoju let him go.

Master Fuoco slumped onto the tatami matting with a gurgling moan, a twitch, and then stillness. Silence followed. The most satisfying silence Shoju had ever experienced.

He spat on the man's dead body—a great hocking ball of saliva, too. "That's for all you've done to so many boys who trusted you to care for them. May you rot in hell, Master Fuoco. Rot there forevermore."

He went to the poor boy tied up not too far away, untying him immediately because Shoju had left the dagger inside Master Fuoco, not wanting it back. Not at all.

"Who…are y-you?" the young man asked with a slur,

one that indicated his drugged-up state. His eyes were glazed over, leaving no doubt.

Shoju felt for him. "I'm here to help you." He untied his hands and feet first, rubbing them to get the circulation going. "My name's Shoju, by the way. Shoju Fa. And I'm a friend."

"I'm Daiki U-Ugomari, and thank you…if what you say is t-true." A tear rolled onto his cheek. "I…I didn't want to be raped anymore, but I had…no c-choice. They were g-going to cut my balls out and feed them to me…if…if I didn't let them make me one of their h-honoured." At that, Daiki began to cry.

Shoju freed him, holding him for the longest time close to his chest, soothing him. "Let it all out, my friend. Then we can go where you'll be safe. That's my promise to you."

More shuddering tears. "Thank you…Shoju."

"You're most welcome."

After a long time, Shoju sighed with relief as he realised one thing. It was over. All he had to do now was get to Osumase with those they'd rescued as quickly as possible, some twenty young men as he found out when outside in the temple gardens once more, thick smoke and flames greeting him instead of the tranquillity of earlier.

A satisfying sight.

Horo helped him with Daiki, the young man still overwhelmed as the drugs within him held on. "Did you have any problems, my heart?"

Shoju nodded. "I only had to kill a demon who went by the name of Master Fuoco by slicing him from his cock to his throat. No big deal…in the end."

Horo smiled. "Good—but we couldn't account for Master Ito."

"What about Master Vitus and the other Masters, then?"

Horo held his smile, one turning more wicked, if Shoju wasn't mistaken. "I've wiped their blood from off my sword already."

Shoju swallowed. "And the remaining guards who defended the temple?"

"The blood was thick this day, including that of the traitor Daisuko."

"Was he the one who helped Mat escape only to gain knowledge of where Osumase was located?"

"Yes, and I'll tell you about him later." Horo looked at the destruction growing around them, the smoke staining the otherwise blue sky. "But only one man got away as far as I can tell."

Shoju became concerned, for that man was the worst of them all. "Then it must have been Master Ito who fled to the village."

"That's my worry as well." Horo gestured for Shin and Itsuki to help him with Daiki. As they did, he added, "But for now, let's only concern ourselves with getting our new friends away from this place."

"Amen to that," Shoju said. And yes, it would be a trek through the forest, arduous and long, to return to Osumase, but he didn't mind.

Not one bit.

Epilogue

The evening was full of as much cheer as there were stars in the clear skies. When the children and younger men went to bed, including Ryuu and Mikaro's first born Issey, Nobira raised his tankard high.

Silence fell over the celebrating and drinking crowd, including those men who'd chosen to remain in Osumase. Kento and Saburo—clearly lovers as they hadn't let each other go, not for a moment—had stayed to join in the festivities, too.

Mat was glad they had.

"This is to us!" Nobira began. "To our victory, to our future, to Osumase, and to our sons most of all. We now celebrate! It's now time for us to love, not fight. And love we will!"

The resulting cheers were deafening!

Shoju and Horo approached. Mat could plainly see the blush all over his companions' faces, the beads of sweat on his brow, too. They'd already fucked, he could tell.

Then again, Mat couldn't blame them. Once he'd announced his engagement, as Horo and Shoju had announced theirs, Akai had taken him into the Moon

Room where he'd been spanked and fucked until he was sore in all the places that he desired to be. Oh, how he desired it. So much so, he'd blown a massive load…three times in a row, too!

Mat loved that feeling.

But before the rest of the celebrating crowd dispersed with their partners—if they had them—to continue with the celebrations, as seemed to be tradition here, Botan and Gorou made themselves known.

It was good to see them again.

Mat came to understand they'd been sent on a secret mission before the battle of the waterfall gate had begun in earnest, not sent away by Ryuu as he'd first believed. What he witnessed revealed all too well what that mission entailed.

The two men were holding hands. They'd clearly become partners—perhaps even Alpha and Omega, too, as Akai had suggested before. Behind Botan and Gorou was the most beautiful sight Mat could imagine seeing.

It brought tears to his eyes, truly.

Not only had his family come with Botan and Gorou, from his parents to his many siblings, all five of them, there was also Shoju's mother and the families of so many others as well. More than a hundred people from Jussei village in all.

With his other hand, Botan held an elderly man's hand, clearly his papa. That pleased Mat most of all. Botan was once more a good boy for his father, together now at last.

But before Mat could rush to embrace those who he loved with all his heart, so glad to see them all that it almost hurt, Nobira announced, "Welcome to Osumase, our new friends and family. Please, we're celebrating here, so why don't you join us! Be merry, for this is a great day. A great day indeed!"

More cheers.

More drinking.

Shoju had already run to his mother, embracing her tightly, weeping like a baby in her arms moments later. Mat felt a lump in his throat to witness such a beautiful thing.

Because not only that, Ryuu and Mikaro had done the same with Mat's family. Mat couldn't help but smile, going to them all, too. He found he was nervous; it seemed he hadn't seen them in such a long time. And as he came to hold his mother, his tears fell. He also cried unlike any time he'd done before, so happy he couldn't contain himself.

He was truly at home now that everyone was here with him.

After he'd given his family his loving welcome, even his youngest sister, who tried to squirm out of his embrace, Mat introduced them all to Akai. Mat's man, his Omega, his wonderful husband to be, was greeted with as much warmth as Mat had been.

This moment couldn't be any better.

The only wet blanket thrown over the joy was when Botan said sombrely, "Unfortunately, Master Ito and some of the village elders are going to re-build the temple, from what I heard whispered in the taverns of Jussei."

Gorou added, "Master Ito raped me the most."

A silence fell.

It was Shoju's mother who broke it. "I think I speak for

all of us when I say we're all with you, and that we're sorry for what has happened. Truly sorry." Shoju and Horo held her tightly. She added, "And if there's anything we can do, just name it. We're here for you all from now on."

There were more apologies, to Gorou and to a lot of them, after that. More forgiveness, too. And yes, the wounds would take a long time to heal for some, including Daiki and the other men rescued before the temple burned, but one thing was certain to Mat: the choosing ceremony each season had been stopped.

No more boys of age would be abused…well, not for a long time, Mat hoped. Because yes, even though the temple Masters had woven their evil so tightly that some of the Jussei villagers wanted to help them rebuild it, as Botan claimed, there were plenty more who understood what had been happening behind those walls.

Plenty more who would fight them, too.

It was Horo who then said openly to all around, "I believe we can begin the healing process by sharing tea together. I'll make my special blend for you all, if you'll join us, please."

But Mat had a question he needed to ask as his family and friends, all of those he loved with all of his heart, were taken to the village hall to celebrate in a more traditional manner before they all paired off. "Um…how will the Kami who've created the nature magic here accept women being at Osumase?"

"They will accept them as we do," Akai replied, his bandaged arm giving off a pungent but pleasant odour of the herbs the healers of the village had used on the wound. "Simple as that."

"Oh."

Shoju's mother, still holding onto him, something Shoju clearly loved and didn't want to end, said, "I've heard that folks can be…changed here so they can become true lovers to each other."

Itsuki said, "It's true, they can be."

Mikaro said, "The Kami may bless those who desire it with a penis, if it comes to that to maintain the balance."

Shoju turned to look at his mother. "Are you…all right with that? If you…grow a dick, I mean?"

She glanced at a man not too far away within the crowd, all hunky and muscular, tall and dark-haired too. "If I can get to fuck a sexy man like him, then I'll be up for anything."

"Mum!" Shoju said, shocked but then laughing.

Mat laughed, too.

As did they all.

His mum smiled knowingly, along with her lovely giggle. "We all have needs, darling. And for me, it's been a long time."

"Too much information, Mum."

Horo bowed once they'd entered the hall proper. "I'll go prepare the tea before too much is said. Please, all of you, be seated."

Akai said, "I think that answers all your questions. Am I right, Mat?"

Mat nodded. "It sure does."

But it was then that Mat sensed something from Itsuki.

A sense he understood now that he'd become familiar with such things recently. "Is there something you wish to tell us, Itsuki?"

Itsuki blushed but smiled shyly, grabbing Shin's hand to hold it to his heart. "Yes…we're pregnant."

And before he could be congratulated by everyone present, Kento announced, "So am I." He embraced Saburo, the blooming love between them clear.

What a great day this was indeed, Mat thought.

A brilliant day!

Ryuu said, "More sons to defend us one day! Excellent!" Mikaro smiled, holding his husband's hand.

Itsuki added, "And even though I love how I'll be carrying our son for nine months, just know that most of all I can't wait to see his face." He patted his stomach gently. "See that he's a part of Shin and me."

Shoju said, "I feel the same."

"What will you name your boy, Shoju?" Mat asked, curious.

Shoju didn't hesitate, "Horo and me have already agreed on calling him Junichi."

"You're naming him your obedient son?" Akai chimed in. "If I'm understanding the meaning of that name correctly, that is."

"You're correct, because that's what it means, yes." Shoju reached over to hold Shin's hand, the action reciprocated, much to his delight. Mat understood they were close friends. Possibly companions, as he was to Shoju. "Because being obedient is not only respectful, it's a strength, too. Mostly because folks underestimate those who are, as Master Fuoco did." The name of the man was spat from Shoju's lips in hate, Mat knew.

Mat understood. "I don't think Master Fuoco, or anyone else for that matter, will do that again."

"They won't." Shoju smiled. "But what about you all? What will you name your sons?" The question directed to Mat and Akai as much as Itsuki and Shin.

"We haven't decided yet," Itsuki replied. "I want something more modern, but Shin thinks otherwise. Don't you, my love?"

Shin replied, "I want a traditional name for our firstborn son. Nothing wrong with that, is there?"

No one disagreed.

But before Mat could answer, tell them they hadn't thought of a name for their son either, Horo entered the hall. He was carrying the tray for their tea ceremony, full of cups and a large pot.

It was then Akai cleared his throat. "I suspect the rebuilding of the temple under Master Ito's watchful gaze has already begun, as I know such men don't waste time, especially if it means they'd otherwise lose their grip on the power they've held for so long."

"Tradition is hard to break," Ryuu replied stoically. "And I know that the elders of the Jussei village will still believe in the Cult of Men, even after they've discovered how the boys chosen to serve it have been treated."

Mat, worry stabbing at him, asked. "What can we do, then?"

Akai smiled knowingly at that. "I have a rather delightful idea I'm sure you'll all love."

"What is it?" Shoju asked. The others gathered with equal curiosity in their expressions.

Akai, sipping from his cup and sighing with obvious satisfaction from the taste of the brew, explained, "I haven't got the full approval of Nobira and the council of elders yet, but I plan on building our own temple. A temple where anyone can come to be respected and learn to defend themselves, as they should be able to. It'll be a safe place, too."

"That's a wonderful idea," Mat's mother said, nodding after accepting her offered cup full of steaming tea that wafted a gentle fragrance of honey and wood.

"It is," Mat agreed. He then felt a flush of something else wash through him. "And I'll do whatever I can to help you with this, my husband-to-be."

Shoju asked, "You're getting married like Horo and me are?"

Mat beamed a proud and loving smile. "We are."

Itsuki said, "As we are, too!" He looked at Shin, nothing but love between them.

Horo, sitting cross-legged at the table to enjoy his own cup of oolong, said, "Then we shall all exchange our vows inside this new temple. I'm sure Nobira will be more than happy to officiate the ceremonies."

"I will be," Nobira agreed.

Mikaro bowed his head slightly. "A great idea indeed, then!"

"Shotgun weddings all round then, hey?" Mat said cheekily, unable to help himself.

Akai looked shocked for a moment. "Trust you to say that."

Shoju laughed, but Gorou said, "I want to marry you in the new temple, Botan."

"You do?" Botan said, his surprise clear.

Gorou then said the most astounding thing, one that got giggles behind hands and knowing smiles from all present. "That way I can take you to our wedding bed afterward so that I can fuck you over and over until you pass out from exhaustion, my Botan."

"I'd really like that." Botan blushed deep red circles on his cheeks. "Honest as I sit here."

At such talk, and being close to Akai, Mat felt himself stir, his erection already pressing against the cloth of his fundoshi, achingly so. "I don't think I can wait that long." He then gulped down the tea in one mouthful, getting up. "And if you'll excuse us, everyone, I need my man so badly I hurt everywhere. So please, let's go, Akai!"

Akai took Mat's hand, kissing it. "I love you so much, my Matashi, for you're my only desire." Tears welled in his eyes. "And I can't think of anyone else I'd rather spend the rest of my life with."

"I love *you*, my Akai, my love. And I love you most of all as the father of our son, too. You're going to be an awesome dad."

"As you will be, too." A tear of joy fell onto Akai's cheek. "And I want for nothing but to die of old age in your arms after a lifetime of your love."

"I want to grow old with you, too."

Mat left the hall with Akai, hand in hand, laughter and

conversation from all of those he loved, his old family and new, in their wake. Tonight was going to be as awesome as the day had turned out to be.

He couldn't wait for the soreness he'd feel tomorrow.

The End

About Kon Blacke

By day I'm a humble physical therapist…and by day I'm also a writer of sweet & saucy boyslove stories (18+). I sleep at night as an old fart like me should. I'm both self-published and traditionally published. Other than that, I live with my partner and two cats and live my best life.

Website: http://konblackeboyslovewriter.com
Twitter: http://www.twitter.com/blackekon

Books by Kon Blacke

Battle for Atashaal
A Cat's Play is the Death of Mice

The Legend of Hereward
Immortal Whispers (Book One)
Mortal Screaming (Book Two)

Boyslove in the Gangland District
Offering Gold Coins to a Cat (Book One)
Soft Boys Play Hard (Book Two)
Catching Two Frogs With One Hand (Book Three)
The Chirping Cricket Desires the Ripened Crop (Book Four)

The Saurian Love Trilogy
My Tyrannosaurus Lover (Book One)
My Saurian Friends (Book Two)

Shoju and Matashi
Warmth From the Rising Sun (Book One)
Cool From the Waxing Moon (Book Two)

Also by Kon Blacke
Published by Dreamsphere Books

Immortal Whispers
Kon Blacke

The Whispering Monks have foretold change to the world, and it's fast approaching. They also speak of the mortals who'll be involved.

Hereward, a lord knight who only worships the steel at his side, as the mad magician Ealdræd has taken away everyone he had ever loved. Wymond, an oblate determined to find his true self, even if it means turning away from everything he has ever known. Beornræd, a powerful magician who fears to love again after the cruelties of his past. Kieron, a stable hand with dragon blood flowing through his veins and is the rightful heir to a realm of unimaginable beauty.

All four will travel their own paths, to destroy their pasts and rebuild their future, as they thwart the evil plans of Ealdræd and his conduit, the immortal Abbot Hosho.

The whisperings continue through epic battles, both on the ground and in the sky.

The whisperings shall continue beyond the aftermath.

As it has been foretold.

Also by Kon Blacke

Offering Gold Coins to a Cat
Kon Blacke

Tachibana Kushano goes to Michael Brock's gentleman's club, Badda-Bings, to give himself to many other men at once. All because his boyfriend, Riyu, orders him to.

Tachibana never questions Riyu. He's his submissive, after all.

But when he's finished, Riyu still isn't happy, and Tachibana doesn't understand why. And as he quickly discovers, he's never been appreciated by Riyu either, even when he's done whatever he's been told without question. As a result of Riyu's anger, Tachibana is then punished, hurt beyond anything imaginable.

For Tachibana, it's the last straw.

The trouble is…how can he recover after being dominated by Riyu for so long? How can he learn to trust someone else again?

But above all, how can Tachibana love someone else, even someone who wants to care for him? Someone like Michael Brock, for instance?

Also by Kon Blacke

My Tyrannosaurus Lover
Kon Blacke

Karl Meddings is what you would call an ordinary guy in every way. He loves his best friend—with benefits—Sagan, with all his heart, and leads a good life. The only unusual thing about his world is the fact he shares it with saurians—the modern-day ancestors of dinosaurs.

But now, Karl's boss, a rather attractive tyrannosaurus by the name of Benedict Tumbold, has an interesting proposal for both Karl and Sagan—a proposal that could turn Karl from an ordinary guy with no real prospects to someone special.

A hero…

Will Karl accept his boss's offer? Will Sagan? Or will an ordinary life be all that Karl's destined for?

Printed in Great Britain
by Amazon